SEMANTIC
BALLADS

SEMANTIC BALLADS

Five Mechanized Sagas for the Modern Peasant

MATH BLUGRAVE

Cogniblem Imprints

Published in the United States by Cogniblem Imprints.

Names: Blugrave, Math Harus, 1972- author.
Title: Semantic Ballads: Five Mechanized Sagas for the Modern Peasant / Math Blugrave.
Identifiers: ISBN 978-0-578-91373-5
Subjects: Urban fable. Satire.
Classification: DDC 813/.6—dc23

Book design by charlyn_designs (Fiverr)
Cover photograph by Math Blugrave

CONTENTS

The Blinker..7

Comfort Object 35

Industry Standard..71

Career Path 101

Period Piece...131

THE BLINKER

THE BLINKER

Gray Hallsoy pumps the soap dispenser in the funeral home lavatory exactly five times without counting, as he's always done in public restrooms without realizing. The green plastic watch on his pumping wrist is fully exposed in the moment, past the cuff of his suit which's been tailored in the muted coloring of a female bird. The watch is intended as a tasteful and unobtrusive accessory, on this occasion as when it was originally gifted to him, but now it just looks like a length of garden hose inexplicably wrapped there around his wrist. Gray pushes the watch up and away into the recesses of his sleeve.

This is the third memorial he's witnessed this fall. Gray's only had cause to attend one service before these, and that was several years ago. He isn't used to folks on his radar requiring memorials at this frequency.

Gray summarily dries his hands and makes his way back to the receiving area. Oriel and Alina are across the room. Oriel's crying and Alina's laughing, but it looks as though they each may have changed over from the other activity shortly beforehand. They're speaking with a large man who looks just like the pictures Gray'd seen of Uncle Hud in the funeral program.

"Oh! Uncle Lonnie, this is Gray Hallsoy," Alina says as she notices him approaching. "Gray, this is Hud's brother, Lonnie." She pauses to offer Oriel a tissue and turns her attention back to Lonnie. "Gray's a friend of Oriel's and mine. We know him from Westcott. Unlike us, he's still involved in business development in one way or another, aren't you Gray?"

As Gray demurs, Lonnie takes both Gray's hands in his and thanks him profusely for attending the service. Gray's uncomfortable with this to be sure, but he also recalls how he himself had behaved at Makko's funeral just a couple months ago. If the death of someone you knew well doesn't forge the most unforeseen fleeting alliances with people you've never met before, alliances in which all the normal rules of social engagement are void and vanquished, then he'd read the wrong psychology text.

There'd been over 200 people in attendance at Hud's service. Because Gray's traveled here with his friends, he's committed to staying for the duration. Honestly, it doesn't bother him. Traditionally, Gray's been giving of his time. Apart from that, acts of piety have always come as second nature to him.

"Gray," Oriel begins, as she draws another wad of tissues from a Bakelite box on a small katydid-legged side table, "Will you join us outside? We ought to get back to Alina's horses, and Lonnie's on his way out now anyway."

"Of course!" Gray says, "It's such a sunny day in spite of the sad occasion. It seems we could hardly honor your Uncle Hud any better than to bask in his memory as we bask in the sunlight."

With that, Oriel and Alina begin to make their way from the room, and Lonnie lumberingly places his arm around Gray so that he's as much as half leaned over toward the man as they make their stately way out to the lot.

Out they go, past other crying, laughing, murmuring, and sighing respects-payers. Gray notices a single fly blinging repeatedly into an upper corner of the expansive hallway. He counts seven people in pinstripe suits, and just as many in graphic tees. He wonders if the dress is dictated by personal philosophy as much as it is by generational culture.

"I was glad to hear you say what you'd said about the quality of the day," Lonnie remarks throatily. He pulls Gray a bit closer as they walk.

"Sorry, what's that?" Gray observes that Alina and Oriel have walked on ahead. They glance back briefly, but then don't bother to hold the door as they proceed outside. Gray and Lonnie are still a good ten paces from the exitway.

"Hud loved sunny days like this," Lonnie expounds. "He'd have wanted us to enjoy it. He was nothing if not a hedonist, and I mean that in the most constructive way possible."

A woman they pass in their shamble stops hesitantly and appears to be about to say something to one of them. Lonnie makes no eye contact with her and she continues on her trajectory.

"The service was nice, but I've always believed that the best place to remember someone properly is in a parking lot rather than in a velvety temple such as this," Lonnie remarks. By this time, they've actually reached the exitway. "Without further ado, then," and he gives Gray a gentle push out the pneumatic doors.

Alina's looking distracted as they rendezvous out in the lot. Oriel comes from around the side of a large yellow camper van which turns out to be Lonnie's.

"It's locked," she says diffidently.

"Don't fret, neicey-weicey, we've got everything we need right here," Lonnie says, gesturing expansively around at the parking lot, the funeral home, and perhaps the highway and road-fringing wood beyond. Oriel smiles slightly and spits out the fingernail she's just bitten off.

"Anyway," Lonnie continues. "It's a bit of a mess in the van there. Four of my brothers and I went away in this thing this week-end past when we got the news about Hud."

In the interim, Alina's pulled her car over and parked it at an angle to Lonnie's van, completing a sort of corral with a third vehicle parked nearby, outlining and subtending an area about the size of a kitchenette. She gets out, arranges a large sheet of corrugated card-board, and sits down on it. Once Oriel joins her and Lonnie himself manages to hunker down on the makeshift floorcloth, remarkably tucking one leg underneath himself, Gray gives a quick look round and sits down too.

Though it's cold outside, it honestly is a lovely day. If you've ever looked down into a cove from an overhanging rock, that was today's sky, in the opposite direction of course. The shallows are off to the east, pale and sallow. You're up to your thighs in chartreuse wavelets a bit closer in from the horizon, just above the strip of car dealerships. When you're above the chain restaurants a few blocks closer still, you're up to your neck in cerulean spume. Here though, high above this funeral home where Hud has just moments ago been formally memorialized, the sky is fathomless. Plug your nose and torpedo yourself down all you like. It's a universe of indigo firmament anywhere you look, cradling you in its vast pressury stronghold from every possible angle.

"If it were me, I think I'd be out of my head with worry."

"Sorry? What's that?" Gray pulls himself out of his own musings. He's been looking at the sky.

Alina laughs airily and places a hand lightly on Gray's back. "It's kind of why I wanted to have a little caravan here with the group of us, before you'd gone. To make sure you're okay and you know you have our support even if you change your mind about the whole thing."

Lonnie looks over from where he's striking a match to a multicolored pipe and gives her an odd look. By this time, a couple of the other guests have joined them in this sheltered oasis in their camper van wagon-circle, and there are about three conversations going off at once.

Oriel gives Lonnie a pointed look. "We're all gathered in memory of Hud too, of course. We're never doing just one thing at any one time, no matter how hard we try." She blinks.

"It's just that Gray's only got a couple more days before he's off on that trajectile to the blinker," Alina explains with a subtle curl of her lip. "Thought the news may have reached you via the grapevine at least, Lonnie."

Lonnie's eyes goggle as he chokes on his pipe. "Ah! It's to be Gray, is it? I had no idea! Didn't put the pieces together!" Lonnie inches forward on his bottom with concussive jounces, trying to get closer. "Amazing! I should say he's got a load on his mind!"

The trajectile is, in fact, a small rocket that Gray is to man in just two days' time. It's a solo mission, but it's believed by most of the associated staff that the job will be relatively brief. Possibly only a day, but certainly no more than five. Still, Gray's downloaded the complete ramblings of Rashaal Wettucks to his new phone, just in case.

"Well," Gray proffers, "I don't really expect it'll be statistically dangerous. The vehicle and staff are on charter from Stellarize, and

I've been on a couple shorter flights with them. A friend of mine's created an entity which is in charge of all the funding and logistics and so forth, so I'm more or less just the payload. A commercial traveler, so to speak."

"I'd say there's more to it than that," Lonnie reflects. "Apart from how safe your vehicle and other equipment is or isn't, apart from how prepared you are or aren't, no one seems to know just what this *blinker* thing is as I understand. After all, even if the dragon's only a jokester with a flashlight and a friction match, so to speak, there's a real element of foundational mystery to reckon with here."

"I'm flying past from about forty kilometers away," Gray relates flatly. "The craft's going to snap some photos and stream some video, I'm obviously going to do the live coverage and reaction. I've definitely got some oohs and aahs already scripted. The mission may go a bit longer depending on the prevailing tone of that initial sally. I'm going to come down when I'm finished documenting it, get to home base, and microwave a frozen entrée and watch something on TV."

The heralds of the so-called blinker have deployed their tidings over the last month or so since the object had first manifested; heralds from the checkout clerk at Harsh Mart to the big transmitters who never appear on less than a million receivers at any one time. The blinker had appeared suddenly in the sky, and had instantly begun blinking more or less rhythmically in more or less colorful bursts of light. Although it can't be viewed from any latitude lower than one along which large animals with long shaggy fur and a layer of insulating fat rove in abiding darkness, it seems that everyone believes they've spotted it at least at one point in the last month, or knows someone who has.

The blinker never moves from the sky cavity it's selected for itself, and it never reorients. The heralds say that it's about halfway between the Earth and the Moon, that no one has been able to generate a detailed image of it, and that it's probably about as big as a cathedral. Presumably the blinker is a secret project of one nation or another, but no one's fessing to it no matter how much the attention surrounding the thing has intensified. The question of deploying a probe to the object, to say nothing of a manned mission, has honestly been a non-starter till now. This outlook is understood as a practical matter more than anything else. To seriously suggest such a mission to a room of business-dress mortgagors with loving families anywhere in any industry would be like proposing the installation of a twenty-acre cornfield in the middle of the downtown business district.

"Yes, Gray," Oriel remarks, "All of that's fine, you'll do all that, but the elephant in the room, and what Lonnie is alluding to, is the possibility that the blinker is nothing that'll be identifiable even from up close, or that it's engineered from somewhere beyond Earth . . . Or that it's evil." She adds this last bit with a smirk.

"That's just it," Gray chuckles mordantly. "Everyone has these possibilities in mind, no matter where each possibility falls on the plausibility spectrum, but no one's naive enough to believe any of it, right? It's classic party line praxis from a safe distance away."

"The obvious question arises then," Lonnie huffs. "Why is it that you're going at all?"

"Well," Gray begins, seeming somewhat reluctant to elaborate. "It has to do with my makeup, and getting it right."

"Oh jeez," Alina scoffs playfully. "This isn't about your drive past Finnick again, is it?"

In fact, it was. Shortly before the news about the blinker began to circulate, the celebrated entertainer and buffoon, Finnick the Clown, passed away. He was a well-liked figure, a bit of a regional icon, and there was hardly anyone who wasn't affected in at least some small way by the sad news.

The reason Gray and thousands of others were late to work the morning after Finnick's passing was on account of the execution of his last will.

It was in accord with Finnick's testacy that a framework was set up on a grassy verge overlooking a well-trafficked stretch of the Happenstance Freeway. Upon that framework, Finnick's costumed and greasepainted earthly corpus was displayed in a glass coffin for all to see.

Every morning and evening along the Happenstance, first one way and then the other, everyone who plies that route powers their vehicle at the highest velocity which an average between legislation and good-sense permits. That morning, however, there wasn't a single driver who didn't slow to sixty-five-percent of that velocity in order properly to pay their respects.

When it was Gray's turn to cast his glance as he powered past, though Finnick's body had a formal sort of inflexibility to it, though the dinnerplate-size sunflower in his lapel was wilted and his colorful polka-dotted cone of a hat was dented and pale, still Finnick smiled. Still his makeup shone.

Finnick's makeup was his stock-in-trade, and Gray was confident in that moment that it would serve the clown well upon that vast and wayworn pearly plane.

"So yeah, basically," Gray concludes. "I want to make sure my makeup's right."

"Huh?" someone grunts.

"Yeah, like Finnick, like us all, you'll only ever have one last chance to get your makeup right."

It's "makeup" then, literal in the case of Finnick, mental and emotional fettle in the case of Gray, that's being alluded to. The truth is, with this stunt, Gray's grooming his legacy, just as he's formally honoring another man's this afternoon.

Uncle Lonnie had sat for the last several minutes without moving at all, and now his face is as pallid as a sack of cake flour. His cartoony pipe has snuffed out of its own accord, and a thin shred of smoke trails into the sky.

"Finnick's dead?" he rasps. A hush propagates along the small gathering situated there on the cardboard sheeting in the lee of the camper van, and a crow squalls in the distance and flaps away.

Maltev Ninko's condominium is one of the new ones that's gone up on the former bird sanctuary. The news media line is that all the birds had migrated away one year and never returned, though it's supposed that a few anonymous partridges know a different version of the story. Whatever the fact, the condominiums erected on the site are each built in the shape of a birdhouse in acknowledgement of this provenance.

Granted, Ninko's condo and all the others here are quite plush. 500 square meters, fully featured, with hugescreen home theater and an infrared sauna. There's a single large circular opening in the wall, tall and wide as a loading bay, which serves as both a door and a window. There's also a small square cantilevered porch halfway up the side of the building that you can sit on and dangle your legs over. Stairs inside lead down from the entry hole to the single commodious room. Spacewise, it's got the feel of an oversize jai alai court.

In the main area of the room at the moment, there's a large stainless steel table which is heaped with piles of festive-looking junk in what appears to be a sort of arrangement, but it's an arrangement whose ordering principle we can't quite define. Around the perimeter of the table are about twelve large rubber trash bins filled to capacity, holding more of the stuff. Ninko studies one section of the table, moves some items from one pile to another, and then walks partway around the table and repeats the activity with a couple piles there. He takes a large handful from one of the bins and starts a new pile, then adds a smaller handful to the same pile. He stands back a couple paces and surveys his work.

Gray's last day at Westcott was the occasion on which he'd first encountered Ninko. He was in a dining hall there, cashing out the last of his account on items in the uppermost third of the food pyramid, when he saw someone walk in with his tablet PC, wearing his signature aviator glasses. Actually, Gray'd just voluntarily tossed these items into a public wastebasket, so it shouldn't have come as a complete surprise someone had picked them up. Still, Gray experienced an odd sensation that this fellow'd just ripped him off.

"Nice glasses," Gray said as the fellow queued behind him. "I've had my eye on a pair like them."

"Oh, they're not mine," Ninko replied. "They're only on loan from Providence. Actually, someone had thrown them away. They're probably poisoned."

"They're mine," Gray smiled. "Yours now, I'd suppose. Not poisoned. It's just that this's my last day here, and I like to make clean breaks."

"Oh, okay. I understand," Ninko patted Gray fraternally on the back. "I think you'd better buy my lunch then too, in that case. Tie everything up in a neat 700-calorie bow for your new beneficiary."

And so Gray had bought Maltev Ninko's lunch, and they'd sat and chatted. Gray was certainly in no hurry. Though Ninko had never asked why Gray was leaving Westcott with about a month of the semester to go, though he's never asked and probably never will, at Ninko's invitation, the two have partnered in several commercial ventures that Ninko's bankrolled up front, as well as a few purely speculative ones. Ninko refers to this latter variety as "bald enterprise". No matter how badly these pan out, and a few have panned out very badly indeed, Ninko is always ready to try another. Traditionally, Ninko's quaffed at the font of opportunity. Apart from that, acts of impulse have always come as second nature to him.

Ninko, it turns out, hasn't ever matriculated at Westcott. When Gray first met him, Ninko claimed simply to be auditing a course on mercantile ethics. Apparently the course hadn't sparked anything for him to want to pursue academia for so much as a single contact hour thereafter.

In his birdhouse-shaped condo, then, Ninko's momentarily diverted from his rubber bins and table piles as Gray emerges from behind a folding rice-paper screen in the corner, wearing what looks to be a bulky pair of jumpsuit pants with gaskets around the waist and ankles and velcro strips on the thighs. The legend "NinkoNaut" is printed down the entire side of each leg in hundred-point font. Ninko's still trying to build a brand on his own first name.

Gray's aspect is a bit drawn. He's got on his own T-shirt which depicts a popular news anchor standing in front of a greenscreen wearing military fatigues. A pair of white tubesocks poke out from the legs of the hi-tech pants he's sporting.

"Ah, now *there's* a pair of space pants," Ninko remarks. "Do these ones fit better than the last ones, or are we going to have to stand in the customer returns line at Harsh Mart for another half hour tonight?"

Gray smiles mildly, grabs a handful of padded mailers from a pile on the floor, and joins Ninko at the table. He carefully sweeps the contents of a single pile into a mailer, folds and inserts a print flyer, seals the mailer, and places it where several others already reside in a mailroom tote box labeled "Rio". There are other such boxes lined up, with labels like "Venice", "Cadiz" and "Tenerife".

"Hey, I might be wearing these pants for five days straight. I want a fit that'll ensure I can knee someone in the crotch if I have to." Gray speaks in a jocular tone, but he's got tension lines on his face.

"Bah," Ninko says, oblivious to the tension. "I'll be surprised if you're gone a day and a half. Honestly, it may bankrupt me if you are. Careful in those pants, yeah? You've got to give them back afterward."

"Of course, there's the possibility I'll die in these pants."

Ninko looks at him like he's joking. "You've already done three quick spaceflights with this outfit we're working with. That makes you a veteran in fifty-year-ago terms. This is why *you're* going instead of me or some career test pilot or something."

Gray dismissively tosses some mailers at him, and they work along in silence for several minutes. This mail order venture is another of Ninko's, and it's actually one of the more successful ones. Ninko has set up agents in several cities that host the celebrated carnivals of pre-Lent. The agents wait until the carnival's finished. Then, just before cleanup is begun, they sweep in and gather indiscriminate samples of post-carnival detritus from streets, gutters, ducts, sluice-ways, and so forth.

In any sample may be found not only flotsam which is related expressly to the carnival such as confetti, prize-throws from floats, and scraps of costume, but also those incidental items such as discarded beer cans, used condoms, cigarette butts, and whatever other unidentified leavings may be present.

This afternoon, Gray and Ninko are working on what amounts to the order fulfillment phase. They apportion the collected detritus into "bijou", "meza", and "granda" sizes, dependent on subscription level, and then they post the material off to subscribers in these padded mailers. In this way, the subscribers can experience the actual essence of well-known carnivals around the world without leaving their homes.

"We definitely ought to develop a company culture that spans these different ventures," Ninko opines. "You think so?"

Gray's not entirely sure if Ninko's purposely changing the subject, but he raises his eyebrows inquiringly anyway.

"It's probably obvious to most people that the purpose of this jaunt of ours to the blinker isn't *research*, right?"

"I can bring a clipboard along if you'd like," Gray laughs. "I'm fairly sure we're undertaking it for any sort of publicity we can drum up at any conceivable opportunity."

"Well yes, obviously," Ninko assents, "A lot of said publicity's already come our way, of course, and I've got other tie-ins in the works. That's always going to be vital to the sort of thing we do. I'll never deny that. What I'm really referring to, though, is the element of *faith* which seems particularly bound up in this trip."

"You mean trusting that the rocket isn't going to blow up with me in it, or just otherwise squaring the fact there's no scientific, political, or practical rationale for this stunt?"

"I'm quite serious." Ninko pauses in his mailer-stuffing. "Since we first flopped onto dry land . . . People, you know? I don't believe we've ever truly done anything of this scale purely on faith. Anything with even half the budget and impetus of this project has always been researched practically to the point of knowing the final outcome before it's even begun. This is literally a faith-based space mission. Not sectarian, but humanitarian."

Now it's Gray's turn to look at Ninko like he's joking. "It would be silly of me to deny I have my own reasons for participating in this venture," he remarks. "As far as faith is concerned, I can tell you honestly that I've had my fingers crossed most of these past few weeks."

Ninko lets out a single chuffing sound which is either an expression of amusement or exasperation, but then he smiles mysteriously.

"Have you tried talking to it yet?"

"Hmmm?" Gray looks up slightly, head tilted to the side.

"The blinker, I mean. It doesn't exactly talk back to you, but it lets you know it's listening. You kind of feel it in your eardrums. They blink along with it for just a few seconds. It's half an actual sensation, half an intuition."

"I generally trust your instincts, Ninko, but I barely talk to the people I see every day. I probably don't have much of a knack for blinkerspeak."

"Okay," Ninko capitulates, accepting Gray's dismissal for what it is. "You ought to know, though, that I wouldn't send you up on this one if I wasn't sure things were all lined up properly with . . . rightfulness, maybe?"

Gray finally laughs sincerely. "You've really got a subversive way of approaching the sorts of enterprises that people normally hire actuaries and financial analysts for. I can imagine you preaching to a revival tent full of tickertape machines and saving every last tin-plated soul of them."

Ninko gives him a quizzical look and jostles another laden bin around the table.

The two of them flinch involuntarily as from somewhere just outside comes the sound of a string of firecrackers going off, followed by a chorus of whoops and titters. After a pause in which nothing more is remarked, the two return to their table piles and kraft parcels.

66 **I** know I learned the other one at bible camp, back before I'd ever accidentally cracked the screen of any phone I had," Oriel remarks. She takes a sip of water and smiles self-consciously. "Yeah, a super long time ago, in other words, so it may not be exactly right, but I know it's worked before the way I'm describing."

"Okay," Alina frowns doubtfully. "So, I hold my nose and shut my mouth, and then make as if I'm going to inhale?"

"Yep," Oriel affirms, steadying Alina's back, and placing her other hand gently but firmly on Alina's stomach. "Then you cough, and then swallow, and do that cough-swallow thing at least five times in a row. Think of this as accessing the hidden service mode on your TV set."

Alina goes through the steps, and waits a long moment.

"Nope. Nothing," She says. "My pulse is steady as ever. No signal from beyond, I'm afraid."

"Yeah, well okay." Oriel shrugs. "All these maneuvers have a physiological component too. They're supposed to detect heart murmurs, check airway continuity, and unstop your ears when you've just gone up in an airplane. Stuff like that. There're a few of them."

"And why're these maneuvers supposed to work as anything other than physiological tests now?"

"It's the context of the maneuver, as I understand. We're thinking and talking about Hud. Also, it's still within a week of his passing." Oriel holds her water glass up to the light and then hastily sets it back down. "It's supposed to have a spiritual component within the week after."

"Yeah, it sounds like a bible camp story."

"It's honestly worked, though," Oriel maintains. "You consider your question, do the prescribed maneuver, and then for just a few seconds, your pulse will beat in the rhythm of human speech. It'll answer your question. I asked Makko a couple months ago, just a day after he'd passed."

Alina squints at her friend with not a small measure of scrutiny and goes back to the prescriptive nose-pluggings and epiglottal contortions.

After Hud's service the day before, once the parking lot had nearly emptied out altogether and it was just them, Gray, Lonnie, and a couple other stragglers, Gray'd taken the two of them aside and given them the key to his apartment. It wasn't that he didn't expect to return, he'd explained. It was just that he saw this as an opportunity to formally divest himself of those items he'd happened to own before this latest tipping point of his. He'd asked each of them to choose anything from the apartment that they were either the most drawn to, or just happened to want or need the most. He invited them to keep whatever it was they picked. He'd arranged to have workers come later that afternoon and dispose of whatever moveable items were left.

To Gray, as he'd sometimes propound, life is a sequence of delineated "tipping points". Some of these are planned and perhaps more formal, others are incidental and suitable for beach sandals. At Westcott some years ago, Oriel and Alina met Gray at the cusp of one such tipping point. The three of them and a couple others, all mutual strangers at that time, were grouped together for a marketing exercise. Gray offered his apartment for the meeting place, and they'd all agreed to meet there. They were to come up with a marketing plan for a subscription series of eight fully-planned weekend getaways, each at a different point of the compass rose, each "getaway" from one to fifty kilometers from the Groff Tower in the middle of the downtown business district.

The evening their group met to work on the assignment, they'd had to sit around Gray's stand-up ironing board on barstools. Oriel had improvised the setup once they'd realized he had no table or other suitable surface on which to record, develop, or share their ideas for the plan. Two of their group left almost immediately once they'd realized how ill-equipped Gray appeared to be, and they went on to develop a marketing plan of their own.

Oriel and Alina stayed, and they ended up talking with Gray well into the evening. They told him about how they grew up in an area where all the houses had at least thirty windows but only fifteen sets of blinds. They told him about how each of them, as well as about seven other cousins of theirs, had been individually mentored by their Uncle Hud for the Lenten season immediately after their confirmation, about how it was a family tradition, about how Hud had no children of his own but had always wanted them, and about how successful all of their cousins had turned out.

For his part, Gray had listened attentively, and had finally excused himself "for a moment". He'd ended up going to sleep, and never returned to them that evening. They'd let themselves out once this had become obvious. Still, Alina and Oriel had become friends with Gray once he'd profusely made it up to them, and the three of them had actually drawn mutually closer over the past year or two.

All told, most in the Westcott graduating class of that year had done reasonably well for themselves. Alina had gone in knowing she wanted to develop a horse boarding facility, and had done so a short time afterward. Oriel had wavered between wanting simply to hold a desk job at a small office, and wanting to set up a company which would specialize in converting everyday-people events like birthday parties, coming-out functions, and weddings into arena-size arena-scope spectaculars, until she finally went to work with a charitable organization which repurposed discarded filled-in greeting cards, matching them to lonely people with the same name as the one on the card.

Gray'd never finished at Westcott. One day approximately a month before the end of the program, he'd tossed his tablet PC and a pair of aviator glasses he'd worn for most of his duration at the school into the nearest wastebasket and went home, back to his parents' house. Oriel and Alina hadn't heard anything from him until he finally came out of the woodwork nearly a year later.

In Gray's current apartment, then, Alina's just finished tilting her head back and to the side and fluttering her eyelids. Oriel has stopped paying strict attention to her patient and is staring at the image on Gray's computer screen across the room. It depicts a park bench under a streetlamp at night with a polka-dot bindle tied to a bamboo stick, not a soul in sight, all in pristinely cinematic photo-edit.

"Do you believe it's true what that guy was saying at Uncle Hud's service, about the wallpaper?"

"Hmmm?" Alina sits up straight. "Wallpaper? Gray doesn't have any. I'd doubt he's ever had it."

"Yeah. You might have stepped out at that point, actually. One of the speakers, some guy Uncle Hud had sung in choir with, said that when you die, you go to the place depicted in your computer desktop wallpaper. Do you think that was a disrespectful thing for him to have said?"

"He really said that?" Alina picks up the program from the funeral, presumably this was the copy Gray had taken along, and leafs through it. "Did it sound like he was saying it for real?"

"Sort of. He even said that if your wallpaper doesn't depict a place, that it's *rendered* into a place by Saint Peter or whoever, according to a consistent set of rules. I wasn't sure where he was going with that. Anyway, the factory-setting wallpapers normally depict pretty nice places. It probably wouldn't be too bad if it were true."

A peremptory knock comes at the door. They hear a cough and a laugh, and then a jangling of keys.

"Oh!" Oriel involuntarily gathers the tabletop salt and pepper shakers and some sugar packets to herself. "That's got to be the workers Gray hired!"

"Shit! You're right . . . Oh, hello!"

The workers have let themselves in.

In their woolgathering, Oriel and Alina have lost track of time, and now the workers are here to empty the place out. The two have forgotten completely about selecting an item as per Gray's invitation. They think at first simply to leave the workers to their task, but then Oriel suggests that Gray will be disappointed if they don't each choose *something*, and so she hastily grabs a red plastic toaster oven and stuffs it under an arm. Alina pulls a face at her, and after a quick castabout she plucks up a decorative boot scraper.

They apologize to the pair of canvas-clothed yellow-booted workers, sidle out the door, and begin making their way down the staircase.

"Hold on a sec," the goateed silver-ringed worker pronounces to no one in particular. "I've always wanted to do this."

So saying, he walks over to the oversize computer monitor and picks it up, yanking the cord from the wall in the process and extinguishing the park-bench streetlamp image. He tosses it out the largest window into the waiting dumpster they've arranged to have dropped there. The thing lands with a crunch, and with a resounding peal not entirely unlike the sound of a temple gong.

"I do believe the Good Lord created this job specially for me," the fellow remarks with a misshapen grin.

'Twas the day of the launch, and wouldn't you know? They've thrown a party for Gray, now it's going to snow.

The launch site is a broad valley called Remron. The earth all across the valley is a medium rare T-bone steak in the warm season, and a petrified stump in the cold. Until a half-generation ago, an annual open-air festival had been held in this valley year after year which 500,000 souls attended each time, a hard cap of 500,000, and which any soul was permitted to attend but once. Most of what'd transpired at the festival, from the second annual to the last, was a methodical verification via several invasive communal activities which mostly involved nudity and self-expression, that no one was in attendance who'd ever been there before.

Remron is surrounded on all sides by wooded and hilly country which Gray is wont to trek in his off-time, wearing a voluminous linen robe, carrying a long staff, and listening to Rashaal Wettucks on his bone conduction headphones. It's in acknowledgement of this habit of Gray's that a few of his friends have rented a wooded cabin in order to send him off with at least some small fanfare in a setting he'll appreciate without having to *try* to appreciate it.

Alina had brought two of her horses, Samson and Rizpah, to canter guests around the cabin, and she and Oriel had spent a good part of the afternoon fawning over the creatures and helping several people on and off of them who had never previously encountered an animal bigger than a cocktail set.

Maltev Ninko and Uncle Lonnie had arrived at about the same time in the midafternoon. Lonnie had driven his yellow camper van, and Ninko personally piloted the flatbed car carrier upon which Gray's transport vehicle rode. The transport vehicle was fully fueled and custom-tuned. It was designated to get Gray reliably to the launch site in the valley proper later that evening after they'd wrapped things up at the cabin.

Lonnie had taken Ninko under his meaty wing, as it were, had plied him with wisdom-of-years and fragrant smoke. He engaged him in a succession of ill-conceived elevator pitches while Ninko had either appeared genuinely interested, or had suddenly remembered to check something or other on the transport vehicle, and each of these reactions in completely random-seeming vacillations.

These two and a handful of others finally began playing a game which involved holding lit matches for as long as possible, and then bobbing for bottles of light beer in a plastic bathtub.

Lonnie'd hit on a philosophical jag with Gray during a momentary lull in the finger-flare-beer-bobbing, during which he tried making the point that there was something inherently portentous about lights in the sky. Lonnie was referring, of course, to the blinker in all but actual name-drop.

"Even when we're sure that a certain celestial light has a 'natural' source," he'd posited, "Even if it's only a radio tower, airplane, satellite, or supernova, there's still an element of the uncanny to it. There's something that's just plain unwholesome-seeming about intent which is conveyed via a luminous beacon aloft.

To put it another way," Lonnie went on, tossing a handful of cheese cubes into his mouth, "Every light in the sky is both an aircraft and a UFO, a signal flare and a star that conveys us to the next Messiah, a nebula and the glowing ember at the end of the Devil's own cigar.

Be careful with whatever it is you find up there, my friend."

Some short time later, Ninko had sensed a metronome-blip in the rhythm of the party. He'd conferred briefly with Gray, unloaded the transport vehicle, and had left for the launch site in the flatbed carrier. Now, not long after Ninko's departure, it's begun to snow, contrary to forecast. The snow's started softly, but has become more insistent.

The snow isn't initially remarked, but then once enough people have noticed, someone quips that maybe it's the blinker itself which's caused it. Witticisms ensue, that the blinker is actually a giant snow-globe which has just shattered, or that the snow is the frozen tears of whoever's spaceship the blinker is because their cover's about to be blown.

Gray's ignored most of it while he's chatted about nothing in particular with one person or another. Once it becomes evident that the snow isn't about to let up, however, he says his tearful-joc-ular-comradely goodbyes to the assembled, and heads out to the transport vehicle with Oriel and Alina. As he removes the snow from around it, it's clear to see that Ninko's managed to set the vehicle down on the stubby post-fitting of a bike rack that's been removed for the season, and it's punctured a tire. There's no spare to be had.

The group repair inside to see if there's another vehicle they can use, but one after the other, the guests offer surface-plausible reasons why theirs isn't suitable, and couldn't Ninko just come back to fetch Gray as this is pretty much Ninko's whole foxhound and filly show anyway?

The look on Gray's face is so abject at that moment that Alina tells him she has another idea, and leads him back out into the snow.

"This wouldn't have been an option a few hours ago, and it may not realistically be an option now," she says, "But we spotted a decorative sleigh in a shed out here that the park district probably trots out around holiday time. It can't be more than five kilometers through the wood from here to the valley floor. In a pinch, like now, I'm sure the horses can do it if the sleigh's serviceable."

Alina and Oriel lead Gray back to the shed where they'd discov-ered the sleigh, and they all have their first good look at the thing. The sleigh is bolted to a wooden slab, clearly not normally meant to slide at all. However, it appears to be constructed with some care, in the way an actual sleigh would have to be. It does have gilt-edged bur-gundy-cushioned seats that look like they might have been retrieved from a Belle Époque sitting room, and there are a couple worse-for-wear fiberglass horses harnessed to the traces, but the sleigh's runners are nicely wrought and the coach is fashioned of well-seasoned oak.

Oriel pulls off the holly boughs and pine wreaths that have been zip-tied to the sleigh's sides and tosses them aside. "Okay," she shrugs, "Let's get Gray to the launch."

It takes about another hour altogether, in which falls nearly another two centimeters of snow, to detach the sleigh from the display installation, get it out to a suitable working area, and to bellyband, crupper, and backstrap the horses into their traces. The carriage lanterns built into the sleigh seem to be the only practicable lighting option, so Gray nips into the cabin to get some oil along with a disposable cigarette lighter, awkwardly acknowledging the few lingering guests who pause in their hushed conversation as soon as they see him, and he nips back out.

"Are the horses supposed to have their blinkers on or off?" Oriel asks, with a final good-measure tug on the straps.

"They're called blinders," Alina replies. "They should be taken off. We're counting on them to react to trees, rocks, and whatever else along the route. This is going to be much more like yachting than it is driving a car. Honestly, I'm going to be relying on Samson and Rizpah picking out the best route in the general trajectory, probably the whole way as it goes."

Finally, it seems, the three are ready to set out. They take seats in the theater chairs bolted into the sleigh and smile nervously at each other. Alina snaps the reigns, and they slip from the clearing into the moonlit wood.

At the outset, it seems like nothing will present much of a problem. The sleigh is properly aligned and sturdy, the horses are sure-footed, and the trees here aren't any closer to each other than streetlamps along an avenue. In fact, someone jokes about listening to the sound of sleigh bells on their bone conduction headphones to complete the effect, and the moon nearly guides a path for them through the woodland.

Some twenty minutes into the ride, though, the trees draw in a bit, and Alina has more difficulty bridling the horses quite to the slower speed she'd prefer.

Soon, they have to yaw sharply to avoid a tall nearly-undetected sapling, and the sleigh is scoured on the opposite face by a scraggly elm. The cladding is torn off, and the lantern on that side explodes in a blaze of sparks, soot, and broken glass. Alina is able to control the horses, and they finally slow to a stop at the edge of a dark thicket.

Oriel, who'd been sitting on the side that suffered the damage, is unhurt. She's visibly trembling, but her symptoms aren't consistent with being in psychological shock. It's at this moment, and it hits the three of them all at about the same time, that they experience an impression of what a truly foolish course they've undertaken. Gray actually blushes, though no one can see, and apologizes. Oriel is chastened. Alina, alone of the three, seems contumaciously resolute about their pressing on. In any case, they're probably about halfway to the valley floor, so they agree to carry on as carefully as possible with the remaining lantern.

They detour slightly to avoid the thicket, and the sleigh manages to negotiate gaps between the gentler hills without trouble. The horses are still a bit fiddly with these maneuvers, but they're quick learners, and Alina is able to guide them well enough physically and verbally to prevent further mishap.

The valley floor actually comes into view as they round another small hill, but there's still about a half-kilometer to go, a rather steep grade ahead, and no good way around it. Without word or signal to her companions, Alina guides the horses ahead. As they hit the grade, the horses are perfectly synchronized and it appears that the animals will be able to control their speed. However, with no even-out to the grade in sight as they proceed, and a slight bend in the gap, Samson's reaction is to try slowing down while Rizpah's is to speed up by about the same rate as Samson is slowing. The horses and sleigh are beginning to rotate ever so slightly as they accelerate, but then the vehicle suddenly jolts and is jarred to a halting standstill. The sleigh, now almost side-on to the lay of the gap, cants to one side and the three hop to the ground.

Samson has fallen to his knees and has nearly upset Rizpah. At first, Alina thinks Samson's tried jumping over a stump in their path, but then she sees the large jutting rock.

"Is he injured?" Gray asks, coming around from his side of the sleigh, but then stops short as he spots a smear of blood on the snow.

Alina flashes him a dark look. She's seen the smear in the snow too, and is examining the fallen horse. "It's not a serious injury. We'll leave Samson here. Horses don't get frostbite in just a few hours' time.

Their legs are all cartilage. We'll make him as comfortable as possible, GPS him with my phone, and come back with proper equipment once everything's sorted with the launch.

They unharness Samson, manage to right the sleigh and, walking now with Rizpah securely haltered, they travel the last few hundred meters from the edge of the wood to the valley floor.

A service vehicle's been sweeping the line of the wood in the vicinity of where Gray would have emerged in his transporter, and shortly after the sleigh and the three distressed, exhausted, but ultimately relieved passengers slip shushingly from the wood, they're caught in the service vehicle's beams. They're all agreed in this moment of deliverance, with solemn pronouncements, that theirs has been the most horrifying sleigh ride anyone is likely ever to enjoy.

The service vehicle is about the size of a gray whale, but it's mostly shiny black with a little chrome at the ends and edges. As it rolls abreast of the sleigh, a book-thick window buzzes down to reveal a slick-haired canister-necked fellow who Gray's never seen before. The fellow looks down at them from on high, and says "Ninko's waiting for you. Hop on in."

After a short drive, though still quite a ways off, they come into view of the launch site. The rocket looks shorter than it did at the prep sessions, though Gray supposes that's down to his own coming face-to-face with the reality of the thing. The *Stellarize* logo is clearly visible from nearly a kilometer away. Though the letters are supposed to look like stylized rocket smoke, Gray's always thought they look like shaving cream. He'd made up a jingle that went "Stellarize your beard away! Blast off those whiskers the space cadet way!" Ninko had asked him never to sing it again.

As they reach the entryway to the vast launch complex itself, the three momentarily disembark and the wind picks up, blowing snow through the openings in the chain-link. Alina places a call to a nearby farm she knows, sends them the GPS coordinates, and arranges to have a trailer brought for Samson and Rizpah. The moon is almost directly overhead now, and daytime-looking white clouds pass over its face, briefly luminesce as if from the inside, and then blow on to obscurity.

Oriel is the first to notice, at about a cornfield's-distance away, a few-dozen people in what look to be chef's whites scurrying here and there within a cavernous concrete room lit by purple halogen lanterns underneath the launchpad. They can just make out a huge perforated plate under which the scurriers are placing small round objects from plastic containers upon a broad low platform. If we didn't know any better, we'd swear this was an . . .

"Olympic-pool-sized burger grill. Yeah." Ninko startles Gray as he approaches from a Quonset hut just behind them. "This is another one of the tie-ins I'd had planned. That perforated layer over the grill is actually thermal ceramic. Ultra-high-temp stuff."

"Oh God," Alina mutters, squinching her eyes shut.

"Yep. World's first rocket-broiled cheeseburgs. Limited supply of 500,000. Hard cap. We've done a deal with Scramfondles, and they're in charge of all the marketing and fulfillment this time."

"That is literally one of the most horrible things I've ever seen," Oriel chokes.

Alina looks like she's about to do something that she'll never be able to undo.

Ninko makes a mincing gesture at them. "Alright, Gray. Back into the transport, and we'll get you all set up. You'll be outside this atmosphere within three hours, away from all this damn snow, right on schedule. Blinker-ho!"

As Oriel and Alina make to get back into the vehicle with them, Ninko bars their way. "Only launch personnel from here on. Sorry. Honestly, it was really nice meeting you both at Gray's thing this afternoon. You're welcome to remain in the hut here for the launch, and I hope you do. Front row seats, yeah? Please make yourselves comfortable. There are snacks in the fridge."

Gray is practically speechless as Ninko bustles him toward the service vehicle, but he pauses to say his goodbyes to Oriel and Alina anyway, and they all manage some semblance of farewell.

The vehicle rumbles away in a fugue of exhaust fumes and scowling taillights, leaving the pair standing at the threshold of the hut.

The ensuing hours might well already be detailed somewhere else, in some vellum-bound notebook stuffed in the back of a motel nightstand, perhaps, or writ in the deep space quasars themselves, but as the rocket bearing Gray to the blinker lifts from the launch-pad and shrieks away through the mesosphere, billowing sunset-colored exhaust as it pushes its way from this sky to that boundless sky beyond, Oriel and Alina watch from their station, gazing up from the parking lot of the Quonset hut.

Once the rocket's no longer visible, Alina retrieves a piece of chalk from a blackboard on the wall inside, and begins chalking letters as big as parking spaces in the empty lot:

GRAY HALLSOY WAS HERE!

When Alina's finished, Oriel gives the legend a guarded look.

"What?" Alina tosses the nub of chalk over her shoulder. "Shouldn't having been here at all be more than enough for anyone?"

COMFORT
OBJECT

{HEROES:}

The figure we all learn to represent in nursery school by tracing our set-squares for his long beard and gluing on googly eyes, Bindle Bracken, gives his name to half the landmarks here in Pteroport. No one knows if there ever really was such a person, of course, but that's all part of the fun. Bracken's history and legacy are always in flux. He's nearly been squelched in the curriculum and in the public imagination countless times over the last hundred years but, like the Rambling Primogenitor himself, Bindle Bracken always shows up again at another campfire somewhere down the line.

One daydeal, back when the planets came in plastic, Bindle Bracken was pitching camp on a gorsy patch of highground at a spot which would one day become the big Harsh Mart on Bilk Road and 57th. He had his gubbins with him, of course. In fact, he'd only be caught lacking once, and we all know how unpopularly *that* story ended. This time, as usual, he had his combination freezer-kitchen-range-washingmachine with him (and how he ever managed to transport that thing from place to place could singlehandedly account for his legend).

Bindle had a taste for popovers and so he doctored up some natural yeast from the gorse shrubs, pulverized some grain in a frying pan mortar, and squeezed some dew from his bandana. Once the dough was ready, Bindle formed up his popovers, set them in his gubbins to bake, and went down to the cistern to blow a bit of skiffle harmonica.

Most of us can recite the rest. The altitude was levitated just so, the gorse spores virulent enough, the bandana dew at the consummate pH, that the dough rose faster than Providence could ever have accounted for. The kitchenrange flew open as the intumescent popovers played Li'l Chemist with their constituent ingredients. When they got to be the size of beach houses and the color of magma, the unfettered popovers broke completely free and bounded down to the lowground like pogo-dancing mods at some godawful ska opera.

There the things cooled and sat for geologic weeks, at least, until some missing-link stonemasons working on spec roughed the colossal petrified muffins out into the complex that would one day become Best Chance Arena.

Best Chance Arena, branded with the name of the successful legal consortium, is where Loudie's sitting right now, actually, with about twelve others. These days, of course, the place is a symphony of concrete, glass, and steel, looking like nothing so much as the ungainly skeleton of a primordial behemoth which crawled, momentarily reanimated, from a long-extinct volcano and died (again) on the spot. The last time Loudie was at the Arena was for his high school graduation some five years previous. He's here today in a smallish purple-trimmed room for a new-hire orientation. A woman dressed all in gold with lips the same color as her hair sits slightly apart from everyone else in the room. She's been squinting at the far wall and looking like she's about to say something for the last several minutes, and finally she does.

"Hello, everyone. I'm Valeria Dao. Welcome to day one of the job I'm confident each of you will look back on as your favorite."

Loudie involuntarily flinches a little at this. The woman smiles directly at him and continues.

"Best Chance Arena hosts some of the biggest names in entertainment, it's true, but it's also a community center, a landmark, and a cultural beacon."

As gold-clad Valeria continues her spiel, the person sitting next to Loudie passes him a note which he discreetly unfolds.

"Do you think we'll all retire from this job?" it reads.

Loudie looks over. The person who passed the note has eyelids which are the same color as her cheekbone shadows, and a nose shaped like a chestnut. She scowls at him. Loudie shrugs.

"And so," Valeria proceeds, "To that end, let's get to know each other a little. We'll go around the room. Please state your name and the job you'll be performing here at Best Chance, and then tell us about your gubbins. What is it, and how do you activate it?"

"Okay, I'll start," the person who passed the note says. "I'm Bree, and I'm an usher. Here's my gubbins." She holds up what appears to be a lit firework sparkler and waves it around, drawing a picture of a lightning bolt in the air. "That's how I activate it."

Loudie winces as the sparkler flashes past his face.

"Don't worry," Bree says. "It's not combustible. It's an *eternal* sparkler."

With that, Bree pokes Loudie in the arm with the fizzing end of it. "It's, like, just an animated picture of a lit sparkler, but it looks real."

"Okay, okay. Thanks, Bree," Valeria intervenes. "Louden, why don't you go next."

"I go by Loudie."

"Okay, Loudie."

"Alright. I'm Loudie. I'm hired on at the box office. This is my gubbins."

Loudie holds aloft what appears to be a tarnished antique spoon, or at least a length of some rough metal in the approximate shape of a spoon.

"This's been handed down in my family for the last couple hundred years at least, every other generation for obvious reasons, and so my mom never had it but her dad did. He gave it to me just before he passed. The story is that it's an intrinsic spoon, wrought from galaxy-forming forces. I'm told that it turned up here on Earth about four-billion years ago. I've come to believe all of that, and that belief of mine is what activates it."

"Looks like it's speckled," someone remarks.

"Yeah," Loudie glances at the spoon. "It's a burnt-in image of the Big Bang, that inceptive blowup, right there in the bowl of the spoon. I'm not sure how it formed the way it did amidst all that primeval energy, the matter timetable being what it was and all, but there you go."

About another twenty minutes elapse as the remaining people in the room take their turn.

Mercy and Fen are a dating couple who are concessions and parking attendant respectively. Mercy's gubbins is a sheaf of photocopied sheet music which she's got rolled into a tube, and Fen's is a wedge of soapstone which's carved into the crude shape of a standing black bear.

Brince Samway is in facilities, and his gubbins is a "little brown jug" complete with a trio of X's on its face which he says contains a working fission bomb. No one is particularly concerned by this, as such DIY ship-in-a-bottle munitions were a fad a year or two ago that nothing newsworthy ever came of.

Charleston, Leston for short, has already been in the working world for a few years. He's an events coordinator and his gubbins is a gray pebble he keeps in his pocket which he activates by feeling for it there.

All in all, it seems to Loudie a somewhat standard collection of people. It's a cross-section of personalities that would be recognizable from a single public high school or polar research base.

The new-hire group has been granted a fifteen-minute break before the orientation is resumed. Everyone else has promptly left their seats. Most are milling about the room, and a couple have left, presumably to go outside. Valeria is in a far corner of the room speaking low tones into a small device which is probably either a phone or a memo recorder.

Loudie glances around twitchily, stows his gubbins in a side pocket of his homemade pants, a pocket which is the exact dimensions of the spoon, and makes his way over to a table where stand a couple tall silver urns with spigots. As he approaches, Bree plucks up a paper cup with pop-up paper handles.

"Looks like they've got mulled cider and hibiscus tea," she says, popping the handles. "Which'll you have?"

"Uhhh, I'll have the cider thanks."

"What are you? A preschooler?" She smiles. "That guy over there got me my tea, so I'm extending the beverage gesture to you." She motions across the room at Leston who glances up from a display made up of photos from previous events at the arena. He grins over at them, and then finds something else to pretend to be doing.

"He's the events coordinator, yeah?"

"I think so. I'm pretty sure he was in school with my brother. He seems okay. Says he's a member of a leathersmithing community in his spare time."

"Uh, okay," Loudie blinks. "Thanks for the note, by the way. I'm just doing this until I can save enough money to complete my bioengineering degree, so yeah. Probably won't retire here."

"Yeah? The note was a joke, by the way, but this tea's nice. We'll see. Bioengineering, huh? If you think people should have better body parts, why not just become a plastic surgeon?"

Loudie gawps, and Bree cackle-laughs and presses him in the center of the chest with an index finger.

"You're not on camera. Relax. Anyhow, we've still got a few minutes. Let me show you a secret way down to the arena floor."

"Alright."

Loudie follows Bree out of the room and along a broad wall reminiscent of indoor swimming pool facilities. They pass a sculpture in an alcove which looks like a Cubist hockey goalie. A little further on, Bree leads him up a couple stairs to a coat check room, beelines past ranks of tagged brass-colored hangers, places her hand on the handle of an unmarked steel door in the back wall, and pauses.

"This is really sublime. I hope you'll appreciate it," she says, and opens the door onto a stairway leading straight down, no landings, through an opening only about as wide as a snooker cue. The stairway is lit from the lamps in the coat check room alone, and Loudie can see about ten steps down before it gets too dark.

"There are lights, of course," Bree says, "But it's better without," and before Loudie can lodge an objection, she leads him by the hand into the stairwell, closing the door after them. They start down the stairs, free hands trailing fingers along the wall as they go.

The first thing Loudie notices is that Bree's sparkler is still lit up in the dark.

"I thought you said your gubbins was a picture," he remarks. "Wouldn't that be like a painting of a guitar playing you some music?"

"Oh, probably. Yeah, it's a light-up picture at the end there. Don't worry about it. Anyway, we're within a structure underneath the tiered arena seats here, or else this stairway wouldn't have any room to go straight down the way it does."

"It probably makes the stairs more fun to fall down in the dark," Loudie deadpans. "You'd get all the way to the bottom in one go." Bree actually laughs at this, and leads on at an increasingly energetic clip.

"Yeah, I found this stairway while I was poking around waiting to do my interview a few days ago. I intuited it must be here, having seen a couple shows at this place. You like Narrow Band?"

She skips a step. Whether it's on purpose or not Loudie isn't sure, but they keep their balance.

"Whoa! Yeah, they're okay."

She skips another step, and then keeps skipping them with a vise grip on Loudie's hand.

"Yeah," she says, interjecting words between skipped stairs. "I saw them play here last summer. They were bad."

Now she's leading him headlong down the stairs, skipping a step every two times, and then taking one, as if her legs aren't long enough to keep skipping every time. Just as Loudie's about ready to loose a yell, fall on purpose, or leave his body entirely, they clatter to the end.

"Oh my god, I'm sorry," she gasps. "I forgot how long that stairway was." She laughs. "We're here, though," and she pushes through a door which appears to be a duplicate of the one at the top.

Surprisingly, perhaps, the arena floor is hardly illuminated any better than the stairway they've just emerged from, but there's a sensation in Loudie's ears of having entered a vast room. Suddenly, Bree isn't there with him, but then a moment later he sees her sparkler about twelve meters away, probably close to the center of the arena floor.

As he approaches and mutters something about their probably needing to get back to the orientation, Bree stares at him levelly from the glow of her sparkler-gubbins.

"Alright," she says. "We had an adventure together. This's the best time for each of us to reveal their impressions about the other,

wouldn't you say? It's more fun than that icebreaker stuff in the orientation. You go first."

Loudie makes an audible vocalization like the sound of a turtle
being run over on the highway. "Ummm, I think I'd be bad at this."

Bree says nothing and stares.

"Okay, okay," Loudie stalls. "I think you're probably a person
who's easy to hang out with, but you're probably just as hard to actually get to know."

"Booor-ing!" She pokes him with the business end of the sparkler again. "Okay. My turn. You're a Macrobaptist who's been strug-
gling with your faith for a while now, you still live at home and don't
get along with the people there very well . . . and your favorite color
is yellow."

Loudie laughs and tries not to appear ruffled. "Well, you're
actually right about the color."

"You're not Macrobaptist?"

"No, I am. Is it that obvious?"

"Well, I noticed your handmade clothes for one thing. That's
pretty unusual, but there's also something about how you carry yourself. I knew a couple Macrobaptists from my school."

"Hmmm, okay. Pretty tenuous, but I'm impressed in spite of
myself."

"Yeah, also the way you respond to me pretty much picking on
you this whole time."

Loudie gives her a look like she just bullseyed his dunk tank.

She smiles. "You're perfectly self-possessed. It's nice."

By the time Loudie and Bree get back to the orientation, the
door's shut and Valeria is back to her presentation. They slip in and
she pauses just long enough to make a normal person regret coming
in late.

The rest of the afternoon passes without incident. When the
group of new hires are dismissed and begin filing to the exit, Bree's
already off to the side talking with the older guy, Leston, and the
facilities guy with the jug, Brince something-or-other. It's as if Bree
hadn't spoken to Loudie at all, much less shared a harrowing episode
with him down to the arena floor just a few short hours ago.

Loudie gathers his materials and walks loosely with the departing new-hire group to the exterior entryway, an old-timey velvet-and-crystal lobby comprising about twenty swinging, rotating, and sliding doors to the outside.

As Loudie parks himself at the bus stop a few meters from the entrance, Bree emerges from the building with Leston who looks to be in the middle of a story which requires expansive gestures and a booming voice. She glances at Loudie and favors him with an equivocal half-wave. Loudie waves back, and then Bree and Leston head the opposite way down the sidewalk. Just before they're out of sight amongst the pedestrian traffic, Bree laughs and gives Leston a shove, and he feigns an injured arm.

Loudie takes out his intrinsic spoon and stares at it for a moment, making no effort to hide what he's doing, and then watches the rush-hour pedestrians flowing past. He's always had a knack for identifying a person's gubbins, and he's only gotten better with practice.

It's easy spotting a child's. At the childhood stage, a gubbins is something with the connotation of a favorite stuffed toy, and at that point it essentially serves the same purpose. He sees several youngsters go by in parental tow. A little girl with a pencil case, a juvenile boy with a toy hammer which makes battering sounds whenever it's jolted around.

It's just as easy with most adults. The gubbins is usually the same physical object from childhood so, depending in part on how it was selected, it might initially seem incongruous. Loudie notes an orthodox priest in full regalia treading past with a rugby ball under her arm and, only a few steps behind, a woman in medical scrubs with a tuning fork stuck in her hair.

More often than not, Loudie reflects, a person develops in the context of a gubbins they've had from the beginning. Consonance is maintained in image and demeanor, and the gubbins becomes an organic thing; as much a functional accessory as the foundational totem it is. These sorts of gubbins are harder to spot. Still, there are subtle cues which identify them. The way they're carried, the furtive signals (glance, touch, and so forth) that a person makes toward them, and (this sounds weird, but) the way the environment and the natural elements cleave to them. Loudie observes a teenager span-gled with about a dozen rings and bracelets, but there's one bauble in particular, a plain silver wristlet he identifies as the gubbins. A man walks briskly past from the opposite direction in a solid-color three-piece suit in whose right inside breast pocket Loudie is sure the gubbins is secreted.

The arriving bus stirs him from his game. Loudie carefully tucks his spoon away, boards the bus, and slowly makes his way to the very back as it pulls away from the curb in a fandango of blue smoke and glowering taillights. A discarded plastic bag rustles in a corner of the bus stop enclosure. "Take heed! Take heed!" it seems to say as another gust catches and buzzes it there against a leg of the bench.

The pine-tall fiberglass statues of Bindle Bracken which stand outside hardware stores and amusement parlours across the country usually get it about half right. The one by the Striker's Union Bowling Lanes on Backhand Boulevard, for example, depicts Bracken after he'd come to blows with Titus Bitters who'd turned down his credit application. The dust-up itself is recorded in the distribution of the Pteroport hot dog stands and drug stores, each of which was begotten with every biff and wallop of that struggle, and so there's not much point in belaboring it all here.

In the aftermath, Bracken, exhausted from the contest, had fallen asleep for twenty years in the bog just off the one jogging path which loops around the office park with the green brick buildings. When finally he did revive, every centimeter of his earthly corpus was covered in peat except for his midriff which's where he'd had his moneybelt strapped. This is the part the Striker's Union statue gets wrong. There, Bracken's only unsullied acreage is the negative space of socks and sock suspenders, which is plainly spurious. Anyone who's anyone knows that Bindle Bracken's footgear only ever consisted of taped-up shoeboxes, and naught else.

Having just extracted himself from a bog-snooze which would have outlasted most mortal kitchen appliances, Bracken repaired to his most recent camp, a clearing in what would one day become the woodsy landstrip behind Tribaducci Shopping Mall. His trusty gubbins, his combination freezer-kitchenrange-washingmachine, stood there just as he'd left it in all its olive green and harvest gold sanctity. He stripped off his garb, tossed it in and set the foam-whirl going, and then went down to the cistern to wash off the peat-of-decades and to improvise a hot towel from some rabbit wool and campfire steam.

Well, as any respectable folklorist can tell you, Bracken's gubbins got stuck on the rinse cycle. The resultant tidal wave swamped a meerkat colony, washed a gypsy encampment down into a complex of suburban huts, and originated the concept of flood insurance. The runoff also deposited a condominium-sized berg of rock and sediment which would one day be bulldozed and building-coded into Bracken's Lee Park, the most arcane public park I can think of, only a block away from Best Chance Arena.

Today, Loudie of the intrinsic spoon sits in what he's come to think of as the "cockpit" of Best Chance Arena, the box office. He's been going on here for a few weeks now. From behind a plexiglas shutter, he looks onto the heavily pedestrian-trafficked sidewalk and sells the occasional ticket. There's no event at the arena tonight, it's not particularly busy, and so Loudie's been working at his perigraphy.

Perigraphy is a Macrobaptist practice which combines meditation and visualization. In the context of doctrine, the practice is ultimately meant to identify the (type of) gubbins your godchild is to one day receive from you.

To initiate the technique, one selects a fixation point, and creates a sensation of "redolent movement" by orienting one's eyes or head in a sequence of motions with respect to the fixation. Usually the sequence suggests walking or riding in a vehicle, or some other movement which is familiar to the practitioner, specifically from a certain timespan in one's past that one is intending to audit for the gubbins search.

Loudie stares, then, at a half-peeled sun-faded decal off to the side of the box office window. At one time, the decal clearly advocated holding onto your ticket stub. Now, half-peeled, the decal advocates only for the holding onto *something*, though it's no longer clear what that thing is. Anyway, none of that stuff about the decal itself is important. Don't worry about it.

Loudie begins his practice, as he often does, in not a particularly serious frame of mind. He bobs his head, making the decal jump over a fire hydrant on the opposite side of the street. He circles the decal around and then dodges it past street traffic with quick side-to-side jerks of his head. He "blanks out" the faces of passing pedestrians with the decal, reorienting his head as necessary. After some moments of this, though, he conforms to a regular lilting motion and begins to mesmerize himself.

As he falls into a full-on perigraphic daydream, he activates his own perspective:

I launch a recollection of an evening when the clouds, as Before, were purple, and the sky itself was orange-yellow. It's the sky of a pre-summer school night at the very beginning of the week. You know the kind. Though the weekend sensations are sublimating in the evening air, they still feel like an inexhaustible resource.

As I walk, I feel a slight ache in the small of my back of the sort one acquires sitting at a ticket counter for some hours, and a hitch in my knee as one receives stepping a bit wrongly on a hazardous trip down a darkened stairway. With my tongue, I press on the Continuity Reset, a small lozenge tucked between my cheek and gum back in Face Value, and the symptoms disappear, though in all other respects I continue seamlessly along my way.

I've selected a Placesitter who languidly paces me off to the side, walking half on the curbside grass, half on the roadside, skittering his outside foot in the small stones and glass pieces which perpetually reside there.

The Placesitter is in every respect genuine, though he borrows his genuineness from a variety of sources. He has elbow dimples, as did the girl with whom I once roomed in this very neighborhood. He wears a tank top with a picture of a zebra-striped aircraft carrier and yellow foam sandals, as did the boy I once rode with in a car to a waterfall every weekend for a single summer and then never again encountered. He has dark shaggy hair and irises the color of kraft paper, as does the person who will one day become my always-one. Taking affectionate hold of his shoulder or twining an arm around his back as we walk feels just as it should. I'd decided to call him Lev, and so I did.

It's just starting in to dusk. As we reach the head of the street that backs up to the jungly hill upon which, after nightfall, radio tower beacons throb and forbidden bonfires blaze, I experience a flash of why we're here. About three-quarters of the way down the street, along a pronounced declivity, there's a house in what they call the Queen Anne style. The place is dark but for one upstairs window behind which glows a light. That window bears the clue.

Draped across the window, obscuring completely the room beyond, is a crimson bedspread. Even from here at the head of the street, intuition reveals to me that it's my own childhood bedspread, though I've never seen this house before. If we're able to Gleam In all the way, I'll be able to verify it's the same bedspread. For one thing, the bedspread's made from a certain proprietary ribbed material, a sort which could only've been had from one department store which has gone out of business a generation earlier. For another, the bedspread's imbued with a sacerdotal taggant. Encoded in this chemical signature is information on how the bedspread can be used by the properly ordained in megalithic rites or in upper-room invocations. I had only ever used it for bedclothes.

As the Placesitter, Lev, and I Gleam In toward the house, we disengage interlaced handheld fingers and pause for a moment. I gather that admittance to the house, on into that room of the bedspread-draped window, will require some systematic formality. Lev corroborates this with a smirk and with a toss of his head. In this scenario, there will be no entrance either by force of physics or by force of art.

Casting about the street and the grassy plots, my eyes alight on the opening of a storm sewer whose grate is covered in a tar-stuck topcoat of granular paving material. Its presence is innocent in itself. The storm sewer's believably located and possesses no discontinuity that I can detect either with my native senses or with the Continuity Reset (which presently reminds me of its being there, intentionally giving off a garlicky-tasting signal). Still, the grate is too reminiscent of the one I'd known from Before, and so I sit on the curb straddling it with my canvas-shod feet to stare through the opening, in order to parse what I may find there.

At first I see hardly anything, only a vague flicker, but then Lev removes his tongue ring, a miniature titanium pineapple, and tosses it through the grate. As the bauble disturbs the water in the catch basin about three meters down, a shimmering reflection illuminates an object suspended within the shaft of the sewer, and then I notice the thin wire tied around a bar of the grate, holding it there. Reaching in a finger and fishing out the wire hand over hand, I discover a soapstone bear figure tied to the end which . . . my father had once won in a dice game and had given to me, and which I'd lost on a family trip the following summer.

No, that's wrong. That was never anything of mine. How'd that happen? Dammit! Crosstalk.

"Hey! Loudie! What's going on? Turn it down, man, would you?" It was Leston Maddox, of course, this intruding voice. Leston, the events coordinator. Leston and Bree had been flirting nonstop (or something) for the last week, though Loudie believes they're clearly mismatched in age, looks, and temperament, and that whatever it is won't last long.

"It's that parking attendant guy's. That's where I've seen it," Loudie mumbles, now almost fully reintegrated into Face Value, discreetly popping the Continuity Reset from his mouth.

"Huh? You talking to me, Loudie?"

"The bear carving. Like the sort of thing you'd get at the checkout of a forest-themed entertainment center. It crept into my, uh . . . thing."

"Well that's great, man. Don't worry. I won't creep into your thing." Leston makes a mincing gesture with clawed fingers and hunched back and leers at him.

Before Loudie can respond, or choose not to, Bree comes along and joins them there in the box office. Her hair looks more angular than it has, and she's wearing an elaborate pinafore with buckles and oversize plastic buttons.

"Hi Loudie," she says. "Want to come along with Leston and me? We're going to try to get a look into Bracken's Lee Park. See if anyone's in there today. You know, just for feels."

"Uh, sure," Loudie assents. "It's not busy at all. I can take my break now."

The trio exit via the elaborate lobby, through the doors which employ every chronicled mechanical solution to a person-sized panel which must open and close. As they walk along the colonnade which skirts the building and turn toward the park by way of the avenue beyond, Leston makes a mysterious comment about stocking up on anti-salmonella antibiotics vis-à-vis an upcoming event at the arena,

Bree complains about how the elderly manager of the floor crew (Mr. Martis) sits in the press box staring at them like a creep while they cordon off seats (He could be naked from the waist down in there for all they can tell), and Loudie tries to figure out which of them is posturing about what. Before very long though, Bracken's Lee Park heaves into view taking up its own city block, and everyone leaves off with any particular thread of conversation.

Bracken's Lee has been a curiosity for as long as Loudie can recall. His father took him there once many years ago before he finally left Loudie and his mother on their own for good. The park continues to draw a seasonal crowd of tourists and locals alike, and it's still occasionally featured on shows whose intros are characterized by rapid-cut images of dark corners and negative-image landscapes, synced to a chimey and disharmonious soundtrack. No one Loudie's ever known has been inside the park, nor have they expressly figured out its implicit riddle.

The park itself is certainly nice enough. It's a lush green oasis of a place with a few pieces of interesting stone statuary, spots to relax, sculpted topiaries, and climbing structures. The problem is getting in or out.

The park is encased in a structure chiseled from a single chunk of metamorphic rock which looks something like a honeysuckle flower. Four petals rest on the ground in a footprint about the size of a tobacco field. The tubular body of the structure rises up from there and tapers roundly about thirty meters up, leaving a sizable elliptical opening at the very top.

The interior's lit mainly through the open top, and by means of several strategically-placed diffusely-reflecting surfaces inside, but there are also four equispaced openings, square in cross-section, at a height which a person standing outside is able to look through. These lower openings penetrate straight through the fortress-thick wall the same width and height the whole way, but they'd only be big enough for an infant to crawl into, and there's an iron grate about halfway through each one that looks like a medieval sobriety checkpoint.

Any time an organized interest has tried either by force of strength or by force of will to breach the enclosure, as invariably covered by network media, they've met with nonsuccess. For some time, there'd been an annual attempt, though general interest and resource expenditure have been waning for the past several years. Entrenchments dug to burrow in, as soon as they're practicably deep, have filled with water, diverted somehow from a sprawling aquifer. Crane descents have, in like manner, been consistently stymied due to a refracting effect described a dozen different ways by would-be breachers who inevitably miscalculate the angle of the top opening and are deflected off the rounded apex of the structure.

Still, several visitors claim to have seen people inside the park, though no accounts have ever reported seeing more than four at any one time. Usually it's only one or two, and the same person is never described twice, but several reputable sources insist on what they've seen.

Loudie himself recalls seeing someone in the park the time his father took him nearly ten years ago now, though he doesn't trust his memory quite enough not to write it off as an artifact of his senses or his fancy.

In his recollection, he'd run around to the opposite side of the park, out of sight of his father who'd been smoking a cigarette off in a designated area. He'd peered through the grate in the far side and had seen a face peering back, obscured though it was by the intervening distance and the grate in between. He recalls the face belonging to a man with dark thinning hair, clad in somewhat disheveled formal dress; a wine-colored shirt underneath a dark jacket. When the man saw Loudie, he said something Loudie couldn't discern, and then took a few measured backward steps. The man then seemed to smile and to make some sort of hand signal. That was the last Loudie saw of him. For all Loudie knew, the guy had made an obscene gesture at him and walked away. By the time he'd rejoined his father and they both took a look through the grate on the other side, neither of them saw anyone. Loudie'd never mentioned the sighting to his father which was consistent, at least, with the typical mode of inter-action between them.

As the three of them approach the park, Bree spots Mercy and Fen standing by the closest opening in the wall and calls out to them.

Loudie's seen one or the other of them around the arena several times since he's started in the box office, but they'd either been on the way to some other task or he'd gotten off on the wrong conversational foot with them and things had petered out. As they close the distance between, Loudie flinches as he observes Fen brushing his soapstone bear along his sleeve, activating the thing.

"Fen just saw someone in the park!" Mercy says, casting Fen a fretful sidelong look. She too is activating her gubbins, rolling and unrolling her photocopied sheet music.

Leston's first impulse is to look through the opening.

"I don't think they're in there anymore," Mercy says, wandering aimlessly a few steps away from the structure. "I checked."

"I've seen people in there a few times," Bree remarks. She alone of the five appears completely unfazed. "Were you guys having a picnic?"

There is, in fact, a sweater laid out on the ground upon which sits a single banana and a couple of the pop-handle paper cups which seem to be fairly ubiquitous in the employee areas of Best Chance Arena.

"Sort of." Mercy gathers up the sweater and the other items, and hands one of the cups to Fen who looks a bit peaked. "We're on lunch and decided to come here for the first time in, like, years."

"That cider's good stuff, huh?" Loudie says. Bree makes a "What gives?" gesture at him.

"It is, actually," Mercy responds, her face brightening. "Fen always has the hibiscus tea but, yeah, the cider reminds me of going to my uncle's farm."

"Sorry guys," Fen says, stowing the soapstone bear. "I'm not superstitious or anything, but the person I thought I saw in there looked just like someone I used to know from way back."

"Maybe it *is* them," Leston opines, snatching Bree's sparkler from her while she's not looking.

"No. No, it wouldn't be him," Fen stammers. "Anyhow, I think Mercy and I are ready to head back to the arena."

"Give me that," Bree howls, grabbing her gubbins back and giving Leston a shove.

"Yeah, Bree and I are actually talking about trading up," Leston says with a smirk, reaching into his pocket and brandishing a very plain-looking pebble.

"Seriously?" Mercy's eyes go wide. "I couldn't imagine parting with mine now. I've had this one for the last eight years, though Fen actually got his in a trade."

"It was a very long time ago that I traded out my gubbins," Fen says, smiling now. "Interestingly, perhaps, it was traded with the fellow I thought I saw just a moment ago. It was at a summer camp when I was eight years old."

"Yeah, I don't know," Bree says, looking mischievous. "I think I'll wait until someone has a precious stone or at least a mature bond they want to trade me. If you guys are heading back, I think we'll join you."

As the group proceed down the concrete walkway leading from the park, Loudie pauses a moment and looks back. He can't say if it was a piece of statuary or a shadow of a face he'd glimpsed through the narrow aperture, but he'd also heard a whispered admonition that seemed to issue from the direction of the park structure itself: "Take heed! Take heed!"

It was hot as eggfry having just come off of the Postmodern Warm Period, and so Bindle Bracken threw the icemaker switch in his combination freezer-kitchenrange-washingmachine gubbins, and went in search of a cask in which to catch the chilly bricklets. He meant to pickle himself in icicles and sleep till dukedom dawn.

Naturally, he went down to check the cistern first. Folk would often leave tubs and tuns there for washing and soaking. Bracken could borrow one and have it back before anyone noticed it was missing.

Bracken heard Titus Bitters while he was coming round Gnarled Oak. Bitters was already in the cistern thrumming a skiffle shamble on his cow-carcass bass. The low tones reverberated off the stone walls sounding like nothing so much as a coloraturist with a laryngotomy. It put Bracken in mind of a lowing beast, and it gave him an idea. If he could loose Redcap Winters' bull in the pasture above, Bracken was sure the creature would find its way down to the cistern to where Bitters' cow-carcass bass surely still gave off a scent. Bracken owed Bitters an unkindness, and if he could employ a force of nature in deploying that unkindness then so much the better.

Well, as any reputable spinner of assembled anecdotes can tell you, Bracken's icemaker had other plans. Left unattended, the doughty machine birthed a floe so prodigious it threatened to cool the sun. The ice broke free of Bracken's gubbins and the artificial glacier destroyed a golf course and ended up in the middle of the interstate. Of course, no one played golf or drove on the interstate in those antwacky days, but that's another story.

The berg also gouged a divot in the earth that would one day become the Pteroport Municipal Turtle Farm from whose stock are drawn the troupers of Cheatham's Cherubic Chelonians. Stagehands are unloading them at the performer's dock of Best Chance Arena as we metabolize, in fact, not a javelin's throw from where Loudie is taking his lunch in the employee commissary.

Loudie's the only one in the place at the moment, sitting off to the side by a painted window with a depictive view of the sprawling Rue Gueule, here in this otherwise windowless room. With a view to homing in on that long lost article of the sort he'd one day bequeath to his godchild, he fixates on the cap of a ketchup bottle and begins gently swaying his head. Before he can so much as blur the edges of Face Value, he hears approaching voices talking more blaringly than they need to.

"C'mon, be honest," one voice says. Ugh. It's Brince Samway from facilities. "How many times have you been swept along into actually building an incendiary device just from singing a cheery cabaret number which lyrically advocates for the building of incendiary devices as you worked? Don't try and tell me it's not at least a few."

"You're a nutjob," another voice says through a laugh. Ah, it's Leston Maddox. The guy's a little overbearing, but he's okay. Loudie likes him well enough. "I really hope you don't think of your gubbins as a functional item . . . Ah! There he is! Good old turn-it-down too-too Loudie! Hey, Loudie!"

Leston approaches and hovers over Loudie, too close on purpose, goofing off, as Brince stands a few steps away looking as uncomfortable as he normally does. Brince is carrying his stoneware jug with the X's. He's cradling it securely in the crook of an arm, and it still looks unwieldy. The glazing's chipped off the jug in several spots, it's two-tone brown and yellow, and it's possibly got a working fission bomb inside.

"Hi Leston," Loudie manages. "I'm guessing all the bunting has been installed for the autumn summit of the Ragweed Enthusiasts Guild, and a reminder just popped up on your screen about hassling your coworkers."

"Ouch, Loudie," Leston feigns. "It was just the one time I had to get the bunting. Anyway, my job involves a lot more than coordinating the resources to paste up paper flowers."

"Okay. We need to talk. Just us guys," Brince blurts disjointedly. "We're all getting comped tomorrow's show, so we should talk now."

"Huh?" Loudie blinks.

Leston gives Brince a patronizing pat on the back. "We've got an opportunity, Loudie. Nothing big. Honestly, it's just for fun, but let's talk about it . . . Not in here. It's not against your religion to go past your lunch break by ten minutes or so, is it?"

Loudie shrugs, visibly and internally, and agrees to hear them out.

"Oh, before we go," Leston doubles back, grabs some pop-handle cups, and hands them round to Loudie and Brince. "We'd better get some libations. Who knows what sort of household gods we're bound to run into along the way."

The twin silver urns stand side by side on a nearby surface as they always do. Loudie and Brince help themselves to the mulled cider while Leston draws a hibiscus tea, and then they make their way outside.

Just past the entryway, there's someone on a ladder tearing letters off the marquee. The sidewalk underneath is an alphabetic litter. Loudie steps over a fallen fragment which crookedly spells "HEED". The legend had read "HERPETOLOGY DEMO".

"Oh, good," Leston says. "I'd asked them to change the billing. How've ticket sales been for the event, Loudie?"

"Not terrible. We've sold about 16,000 out of the 20,000 seats."

"Okay, well prepare for a busy afternoon. We're going to sell out." Leston gives the ladderbound rune-setter the universal gesture of approval, and the trio continue down the sidewalk.

They soon draw abreast of one of the paid parking lots. There's an attendant milling around in a reflective vest with his thumbs looped on either side of a coin belt. Leston calls to the attendant and he approaches.

"They make you guys wear coin changers, huh? Anyone still pay that way?"

"It's just invisible waves shooting around anymore, totting up the changes in fortune," the attendant chuckles, staring intently at Loudie who hasn't said anything. "These coin changers are empty, but they're part of the uniform." He flicks the spring levers on his coin barrels, and they make a sound like the plunger on a mechanical pinball machine.

"Isn't Fen usually on duty around this time?" Leston asks. "Is he off today?"

"He had to leave early," the fellow reports. "I came down from the next lot over. He'll be back tomorrow."

"Oh." This from Brince. He suddenly looks like a NinkoNaut who's just discovered a rip in his suit. "I almost forgot. C'mere."

He leads Loudie and Leston across the lot and the attendant follows. "I think Mercy and Fen parted company today. I saw them here on my way in. What d'you make of that?"

He points to a patch of tarmac straddling one of the painted lines of a parking space. There's a roughly circular shape there with spattered edges, about as big around as a throw rug. It's darker than the surrounding tarmac, and it looks wet though it's already been there for hours.

"No!" Loudie stands gape-mouthed. "There's no way!"

This sort of thing has certainly happened a few times in Pteroport, and it's a generally acknowledged thing. Loudie certainly understands what it denotes. Though I may not go so far as to call it a "phenomenon", it is something of an oddity. I've heard instances of it referred to both as a "dismal nimbus" and a "doleful corona".

I'd witnessed a similar breakup in a Harsh Mart parking lot a few years ago. The couple stood face-to-face, transfixed upon one another. As I walked past them on my way to the bus stop, not trying particularly to do so, I heard some terse and irrevocable words exchanged, saw quivering lips and protective body language, and beheld the swift undoing of a thing that had taken several agonizing months to build from the dubious foundation of a run-of-the-mill greeting at a hallway drinking fountain.

I'd returned from lunch some two hours later. The former couple was long gone, but a roundel of tears was still clearly visible on the pigeon-gray pavement where before there'd been none.

That hateful halo never dried up. The emotional perfect-storm of the shed tears seemed to have permanently sealed them there into the parking lot.

When the lot was finally jackhammered for a redo, the tear aureole was carefully removed and mounted in the lunchroom of that Harsh Mart as a monument to romance departed.

"They seemed so perfect together," Loudie remarks to no one in particular, having somewhat recovered himself.

Leston slaps him on the back. "If compatibility doesn't kill a relationship, nothing will."

The unlikely group continue on their way. As soon as they're out of sight of the lot, Brince gets visibly keyed up.

"Loudie, you've gotta sneak in on Martis tomorrow and get some pics of his gubbins," he blurts.

"Whoa! What?" Loudie looks to Leston who appears to be stifling a laugh at Brince's expense.

"I don't think you've heard about it yet, Loudie, but Bree was let go this morning."

"What? Seriously? I can't take much more of this day."

"Yeah," Leston continues. "Apparently Mr. Martis, you know, the floor crew guy who's always in the press box, told Bree her services were no longer required. No notice or reason given. I guess Martis is an executive. He's been there forever, at least as long as Valeria Dao."

"Oh hey, look!" Brince again, from out of nowhere. "It's the Self-Abuse Dojo!"

They happen to be walking past Henk Farning's Self-Offense Dojo. Farning himself is standing out front in a gi, smoking a cigarette. He flashes them the universal gesture of insolence, puts out his cigarette, and goes back inside.

"I've often wondered about that place," Leston smirks. "Is it for people who are blackbelts five times over and sick of the whole discipline as it stands? I mean, kneeing oneself in the nads *would* present a technical, spiritual, and stylistic challenge for even the most double-jointed of initiates!"

"It would be better if it was!" Loudie says, in spite of the preceding news. "It's a group treatment place where people take turns calling each other names and generally not being very nice to one another. Like karate-themed primal therapy, as I understand."

"Hmmm. I think I like 'Self-Abuse Dojo' better," Leston mutters.

"So then," Loudie rallies himself. "What's this about Martis and photography? Sounds terrible."

"Yes, it's a mission, Loudie, should you choose to accept." Leston visibly warms to his theme. "Bree thinks the reason she was let go is because Mr. Martis has an illicit gubbins there with him in the press box. She saw it, and he saw her see it."

"Uh, okay. What does he have?"

"I'll give you all the deets later, before everything has to happen of course. In short, we need photographic evidence. We're all Bree's friends, yeah? We want to bring her back, or at least get her the restitution she deserves?"

"Who knows," Brince stutters. "Bree may even give you a big smooch of gratitude."

"Loudie doesn't like women like that, Brince," Leston groans. "Do you, Loudie?"

Loudie smiles and shrugs. "I can deal with gratitude. Anyhow, you're talking like I'm the one who's going to have to snap the shot."

"Well," Leston says with a wry smile, "Your intuition is as infallible as ever."

"We're coordinating a small upset mid-show tomorrow that'll get Martis's attention," Brince interjects.

"Yep. Squib going off near the lightboard. Nothing serious. Just enough to let you get in there, snap your shot, and nip out without being identified."

"Okay," Loudie pauses on the sidewalk. "This is all very cloak-and-dagger if it's not a practical joke. 'Illicit' as in embarrassing, or as in prosecutable?"

"Oh, it's highly prosecutable. Look, I know I don't have a buy-in from you yet, Loudie. I didn't expect I would at this point. I just wanted to bend your ear now before you left today. Reach out to Bree in the meanwhile if you're able and get her side of things. I'll ride the bus with you when you head out tonight and explain the rest."

By this time, they'd come back around the opposite end of the arena. The show trucks are still being unloaded at the dock.

Stagehands are disappearing through the overhead door with ferns and other large leafy plants, as well as something that looks like a prop volcano. Valeria Dao is standing off to the side, observing. She sees the three of them and waves.

As they round the corner back to the entryway, they're greeted with a not inconsiderable lineup at the box office. A ticket-seller makes eye contact with Loudie through the plexiglas and gestures frantically at him to get inside to help out.

"What'd I tell you, Loudie?" Leston beams. "Go on in. Careful of those repetitive strain injuries!"

"Oh no," Loudie remarks as he gazes at the marquee with its meter-tall letters. The legend now reads:

TURTLE ORGY! ONE NIGHT ONLY!

{TURTLES:}

I launch a recollection of the old Mayfold Recreation Center. Have you ever taken a field trip to the indoor swimming pool there? I have, three times over the course of my public school career. It was formerly a site of cultural preservation, but the agencies and leagues concerned with the site's guardianship had one by one fallen by the wayside, and it's been left to molder for a generation or two. Of course, that didn't stop the field trips.

Here I am at the Mayfold, then, experiencing it in the only condition I've ever experienced it in. It's just another stop in the admittedly roundabout search for the gubbins I must one day confer.

The Mayfold, incidentally, was most popular just after the Third Big Change in the popular music preference between the dawn-of-maneaters and today was fully effected. Bindle Bracken personally ushered in the Fifth Big Change, so that should tell you something of the place's antiquity.

Anyhow, the tableau in front of me now is one which has always sprung immediately to mind from those field trips. Having first stepped from the velvet-seated charter bus, it's coming face-to-face with that yawning covered arcade. The arcade's a cross between a cave opening and a proscenium arch. It's been painted and repainted in another metallic color every hundred years. Plumbum for a hundred, lodestone for the next hundred, and argent for the last hundred, till now where it's flaked and chipped into a brazen leopardskin arching overhead. You'd tramp your way into the arcade through that vast drafty aperture, into and out of an obscure and water-drippy interstice, in order to visit the pool room. It had always seemed to me like some pageantry of being reborn as a webbed gilled thing.

The pool's what I've come to see, I reckon. Whenever I'd come with the public school, the chaperone would have gone ahead and cleared away all the crypt-thick cobwebs from the arched arcadeway on into the swimming pool chamber itself with an especially large telescopic-handled rake that was always left by the entryway there.

As I Gleam In, now as on the field trips, the first thing I notice in the pool chamber proper are the hanging lanterns. The brochures say there are 538 of them, but Yan once counted them the whole time we were there. He counted three times and got 611 each time.

I thought I'd forgotten about Yan. I'll make him a Placesitter now, only I'll give him Paolo's hair color and Lara's circumspection. Anyway, I can use the help here. I'll still call him Yan. I'll task him with clearing any errant cobwebs further in, and have him belt out a few canzonettas from Before. The acoustics in here are great.

In any case, the lanterns hang on chains long enough to bind entire pinkball teams to one another. There isn't a duplicate among the lanterns in design, their blown glass globes represent every color and shape, though most of them look like they've come from the same land that curved swords and musclebound folk-spirits have.

The lanterns haven't been lit since the planets came in plastic, but the fractured prism-mirrors set flush with the ceiling diffuse enough light to see by if it's the least bit sunny. The chaperones wouldn't take us at all unless the meteorology charts for the day received the most auspicious rating.

I may as well just tell you that the thing everyone mentions about the swimming pool afterward is the shape of the room it's in. In cross-section, from side-on, the room's a rhombus, so that when you enter from the arcadeway, the ceiling slants up (if you're "graphing" the cross-section from the west, my left as I enter the pool room, the slope of the ceiling is -1/2) to a rectangular far wall across the pool; a wall of strikingly monolithic vertical dimension. All the walls of this room are plumb. It's the ceiling and pool bottom (as well as the very foundation of this part of the building) which are slanted parallel to each other and complete the rhombohedron of the room. The floor surrounding the pool is flat, thankfully, and the pool's interior comprises a shallow end at the far side of the room, ramping down parallel to the ceiling thirty meters above, to a very deep end at the near side. Unsurprisingly, the pool is now empty of water.

This rhomboidness is especially interesting to note this time, because there's a door on the far wall that's the same height up the wall as the difference in *relative* height between the facing walls on the near and far end of the room. From (flat) floor level, the door's just about twelve meters up the wall. I've never noticed the door before, and it's probably because it was never there. It's as if the door had been at floor level at a former time (maybe even *below* floor level before that), and some giant machine had pulled the far wall up while all three pairs of facing surfaces of the room remained parallel, forming the rhombohedron. Of course, the floor around the pool kept stationary. Such a maneuver would've been structurally impossible even if all the relevant edges had been hinged. We're probably meant to presume that if the room's vertices were all (or had remained) at right angles, the door would be at floor level as normal.

I wander across the room, skirting the vertiginous pool-opening to investigate a loose piece of paper on the floor underneath the precipitous door. It's a piece of graph paper on which, about fifteen years before, I'd drawn a blueprint of my room. I was plotting where the organ-growing tanks would be installed in that austere wood-and-plaster chamber of mine. My earliest childhood crayon drawings were done on graph paper, as it happens, and I've written my last testament on the stuff too. Finding my blueprint here is more than enough for me to go on.

I call Yan over to alley-oop me to the door by way of the McCreegan belaying technique. He does so, no crash no rash, no questions asked, all without a break in the current canzonetta he's squeezeboxing from his iron-plated lungs. Oddly, perhaps, I have no problem reaching the twelve-meter door, right up until I get chest-level with the bottom of it. From there, I practically sunder my scaphoids finessing myself onto the placemat-wide threshold. I make it, though. At this point, my intuitions are following *me*. I turn the scuffed housewares-shop doorknob and walk into . . .

My childhood bedroom. The large window is to my right, accurately so, and the crimson bedspread which drapes it rustles gently in a midafternoon breeze from my childhood backyard. The smell of honeysuckle from the shrubs outside is unmistakable. My room is totally bare-bones and ascetic. A rough wooden desk, a ladder-back chair, and a candle stub by whose light I'd do my homework are the only appurtenances. My father's supercomputer was a floor below.

When he ran his calculations, it would shake the aluminum stage of the one item of tech fetish I'd owned; Electric Ballet. Electric Ballet had the entire company of the Stushevatsya Ballet in painted miniature on bases with vibration-sensitive prongs underneath. When the supercomputer ran, the company would incidentally reconfigure before I even had them arranged for the prologue, and it was an endless source of frustration to myself.

There are lines of tape on the particle-board floor marking out where the organ-growing tanks would go once I'd saved enough money. By the wall across from the window, there are two rings of tape on the floor that don't belong. They're perfect circles, same size and shape, taped out side by side. I look to the window, see something stirring beyond, and then look back at the tape marks. This time, the two silver urns are there, each one stood within its circle.

Wow. This crosstalk's getting weird.

A rhythmic hammering starts in. As first I figure it's my father's supercomputer working on a calculation from the floor below, but then Yan signals to me, his head popping up from the foot of the open door where I can still glimpse the Mayfold pool room. Even now, Yan's mid-canzonetta. He points to his ear and makes a walking gesture with the "V" fingers of his other hand. I want to finish out the perigraphy, this is a pretty important node I've reached, and so I repeatedly mash the Continuity Reset with the muscular tip of my tongue. The hammering fades for a moment, but it's ultimately no good. Face Value wants its dinner right now. I perfunctorily extract the Continuity Reset from my cheek, paste a neutral-looking smile on my face, and renounce my own perspective.

It's Bree, banging on the box office plexiglas with the flat of a rhinestone handbag.

"Hey Loudie," she says. "I'd like to talk with you for just a bit if you don't mind."

"Oh, hey Bree. No, of course I don't. Come on in."

Loudie dazedly walks round to the entryway and pops the crash bar on the nearest door. Bree scurries in and scans the lobby to make sure she hasn't drawn the wrong sort of attention. The lobby's empty and fairly quiet, save for the plinking of an electronic directory kiosk and the muted audio from the event going on from deeper in the building. The show has been in progress for almost an hour now.

Bree unconsciously draws a lightning bolt with her sparkler, as Loudie looks on with some bemusement.

"I'm not sure what all Leston told you about why I was let go yesterday."

"Not much in the way of detail. I mean, I wasn't being nosy, but you know how Leston can be."

"Right. Which is why I wanted to stop by and actually tell you goodbye."

"Well," Loudie begins awkwardly, "Leston's got a plan to get you back in. I thought maybe he'd have discussed it with you."

"Of course he does." Bree raises her eyebrows skeptically. "Honestly, I don't need his help. Whatever Leston's told you, I'm fairly certain after yesterday that each of those silver urns are gubbins. The tea one's Martis's and the cider one's Dao's. Can you guess how they're activated? Anyway, look, that's not why I'm here. Tell you what, I'm going to kiss you, okay? It's the last chance."

Loudie's already leaning back against the directory console as Bree moves in and plants a firm and lingering kiss full on his mouth. To be polite, Loudie does his best to return the kiss. Finally, Bree pulls away and they both look at each other for a moment, neither of them speaking.

Not knowing quite else what to do or say, Loudie blurts "You should check out the show. No one'll notice now that it's underway. You can use the secret stairway down to the floor."

"You think I should?" Bree scrabbles in her handbag and pulls out a tube of lip gloss which she begins applying.

"Yeah, of course. I'll be checking it out shortly myself from back of the loges. Tickets have sold out, so nothing really for me to do out here. I just have to secure the box office is all."

"Okay," she says listlessly, capping the lip gloss. "I've heard a little about the show so I'll take a quick peek out of morbid curiosity. I probably won't stay long."

"Great. Okay, then. Goodbye, Bree. Who knows? Maybe Leston's plan will work and you'll be back."

Bree laughs airily and turns on her heel. "Goodbye, Loudie," she says, and heads for the interior hallway.

As soon as she's out of sight, Loudie checks the large brass clock on the opposite wall. He'd have to pop in on Martis in about twenty minutes' time. He'd better grab the camera Leston supplied and get up to the press box so he'd be ready for the signal. He idly picks up a playbill from the night's performance which has been left on a side table and turns over the flyleaf:

One hundred (Count 'em! One hundred!) hormonal turtles have been specially selected from the stock of Cheatham's Cherubic Chelonians' most seasoned performers. They've been chosen for size and stamina, and pheromonally primed for this evening's event which is scheduled for an uninterrupted six hours. All ticket holders are entitled to each and every hour of the six. Our staff herpetologists tell us that turtles make it last, and our arena spectacular promises to keep pace.

Loudie puts the playbill back right where he found it, adjusting the angle to conform as closely as possible to its undisturbed position. He pushes through the lobby doors on into the interior hallway.

Some minutes later, Loudie's installed himself in back of the press box. Its exterior is unlit, but a dim light shines from beneath the door. Leston's assured him that it's only ever Mr. Martis in the box, even during the most popular shows. If members of the press *are* invited, there's a roped off section of seats near floor-level that they're put in. The press box is halfway up the tiered seats. It's a completely enclosed room that looks directly out to the arena from windows in front. There's a thick columnar support element just off to the side, and between this element and the wall of the press box, there's a vertical opening about a half-meter wide which looks directly into the arena. It's here that Loudie stations himself in preparation for his task.

Loudie peers through the opening and identifies the lightboard in a small booth off to the side at floor level. He has a direct view, so he takes out the light-colored chamois cloth Leston gave him and waves it over his head for several seconds. He receives a return chamois-wave from the lightboard, and so he takes a few deep breaths, checks his camera is properly set, and he gazes around the arena.

The floor has been completely redesigned to resemble a Triassic seaboard. There are muddy hills, ferns and vines, fronded trees, and even a smoking volcano off to one side. There are also colored lights whirling across the scene, lasers of various colors, electronic dance music laden with the sounds of insects and lizardine vocalizations, as well as the occasional swooping shadow of a flying reptile projected from somewhere above.

Of course there are a host of turtles: a pair or trio of them covering most individual features of the scenery; a hundred altogether if the playbill is to be believed.

Loudie looks around at the audience filling nearly every seat in the house. Most are staring intently at the arena floor, and some are snacking on popcorn and candy, whispering back and forth with the people sitting next to them. There's honestly more than one spectacled person with graying temples wearing a tweed jacket with suede elbow patches who's taking notes. There's even a pair of teenagers sitting in the very back row, not two meters from Loudie's bolthole, who are unabashedly making out.

The flash and bang when they come catch Loudie off guard. There's no discernible interruption in the show itself, but several audience members have noticed the apparent mishap over at the lightboard. Loudie rouses himself as from a dream. He hares around to the press box entrance, flings the door wide, and manually snaps off about five shots before he freezes.

Loudie really can't move. Perhaps it's a physiological artifact; some sort of spasm, or maybe even a stroke. Loudie feels no pain or any particular physical sensation, but he's compelled to watch as Mr. Martis turns slowly around to face him. It's as if the man's standing atop a rotating dais. The dark suit Martis wears can't be the same one as Before, can it? Still, the wine-colored shirt looks just as Loudie remembers. Martis is considerably older, of course. Wisps of downy white hair seem to float about his head and he's somewhat thinner, but there's the look of realization in the eyes, just as Before. Now, the ambiguous smile forms once more, and a hand raises again in the gesture which is something like a beckoning and something like a warning.

In a split instant, immense rays of irresistible light and heat emerge from the man's face. Not just the man's face, they emerge from everywhere. There is a sound like the ocean being torn in half. Loudie sees every color at the same time, experiences a simultaneous thumb-hammer and tender caress in each nerve, and is instilled with a lifetime of breaths in one.

Everything goes slack.

"Those poor turtles," is the first thing Loudie hears when he can hear again. It's Mercy from concessions, but they're not in the arena. He waves a greeting to her indistinctly. At first, Loudie has no idea where he is. He's never been here before. But then, all at once, he knows. He's standing in a lush patch of grass which comprises a sizable area about as extensive as a tobacco field. On every side, smooth rock surfaces stretch up to an elliptical opening high overhead through which sunlight flares. He looks slowly round, and identifies the square openings, too small to pass through, one in each of the four upcurving walls.

Mercy's there, gazing through one of the openings and muttering about turtles. Brince Samway is also nearby getting sick in a topiary, sobbing and saying something like "It was an accident. I didn't mean to. I only meant to activate my gubbins," between subsequent bouts of retching. Valeria Dao is there too, looking perfectly composed and sitting casually on a stone bench. In the same sort of momentary panic one experiences when one believes they've lost their keys, Loudie realizes that his gubbins, the intrinsic spoon, is not there. He pats his special pocket, and scans the ground all about. It's gone. As he looks around at the others, they too appear to be bereft of theirs.

In the moment, Loudie notes mordantly and involuntarily that, of the Best Chance staff he'd have considered friends of his, about a full half of the arena's workforce altogether, none of the people here make up that half.

Loudie wanders over to Valeria Dao. "What the hell?" is the only thing he can think to articulate. At first, she seems to have no response. After a moment, though, she looks at him earnestly.

"What we'd always hoped for," she articulates, "Was not an assurance that the one thing we almost always had close at hand would save us from ourselves or from any other calamity. Quite obviously it didn't. What we strove for was continuity. Something like our own arm as long as it was still attached, or our unshakable conviction that we were in the right on prom night in the party room of the all-night restaurant.

Once we're assured that continuity abides, that we'll never be completely abandoned by it, we understand that any gubbins is just another one of the realm's natural features."

There's a brief scrabbling, someone flips on the overhead fluorescents, and we all contort our eyes as our retinal cells reenact some famous battlefield skirmish with the blitzkrieging photons.

So that's just how it happened, class. That's how Bindle Bracken received his gubbins. Best Chance Arena was blown to smithereens by an ill-conceived comfort object, the press box was ejected and cast clear to a hobo camp on the outskirts of town, and a couple home appliance artisans who owed Bracken a kindness set to work on it with evaporator coils, heating elements, and spin assemblies. By the dawn of the next day, it was finished. Bracken's combination freezer-kitchenrange-washingmachine, fueled on propane and paradox, effectively landed right at his feet.

Or isn't that the way you'd heard it told?

INDUSTRY
STANDARD

"The openings in chain-link are shaped like diamonds. It's like walking through a curtain of diamonds. Just think of that while you're stepping over a pile of moldy textiles or threading your way around a sprung chair just on the other side."

Jad Filo and Yenni Mender slip through a gap in the fence, on into the junkyard. Here, a mass of brittle plastic pipes the size of smokestacks and in a variety of surprisingly vivid colors are stood on end, arranged somewhat like the ramparts of a cartoon fortress. With scarcely a thought for any hidden defenders who may be lurking, the two pass through to the moguls of castoff chattels beyond.

"Yep, you're a nudger through-and-through, Jad." Yenni smiles amusedly as she watches the fastidious way Jad picks through a ziggurat of shattered milk crates. Jad, balanced shakily atop a hollowed-out TV set and scrabbling toward someplace above, looks back at her and taps the nudger badge on his chest in mock reverence.

While performing their professional work, Jad and Yenni articulate with one another, as nudgers and flaggers typically do. Yenni's the flagger in this equation, and she and Jad belong to the same TotalTong known informally as "Bond Barbian and the Blond Barbarians". Bond Barbian is a real person, the topper of Jad and Yenni's TotalTong in fact, but the official designation of their organization is only alphanumeric, and it achieves an identification which, though regulation-unique, is evocative only of nameplates, employee manuals, industry awards, and other administrative pap. The unofficial names, the ones anyone ever knows a TotalTong by, are usually established early on, after hours, around campfires or fight-pits.

Yenni leaves Jad to a slow-motion pole vault of some particularly foul-smelling carpet-rolls, or whatever it is he's doing, and follows the path recorded on his positioner from the last time he was at the place.

"Yeah, it's not over here," Yenni hears him call, just as an aperture in the piles of debris opens in front of her onto a plausibly structural-looking mound. It actually does resemble a "Tupperware mega-lith", just as Jad had described it to her a few days ago.

"This looks like it must be what you're looking for here," she calls, but then already hears the rattling of Jad's spraycan as he approaches, having slid gingerly down the face of a slowly-cascading wall of mismatched boots, expired phonebooks, and plastic guitars, all in various stages of decomposition.

"Yenni!" he exclaims, "That's it! Fantastic! You're the devil's mouthwash!"

Jad shakes his spraycan vigorously, and sprays a test line on some solid-looking junk at the base of the structure. What comes out is a spiky-looking cloud of . . . something. Not paint, exactly. The spraystuff looks silver and reflective from some angles, flat dull blue from others. It fades in a few seconds leaving no visible trace, but Jad and Yenni have their imaging specs on, and they can see what Jad's rendered. It's a simple yet precise curlicue. A signal to someone with the ability to receive it. Jad flips his spraycan to auto and waits for a reply.

The spraystuff is an electromagnetic aerosol which a whole cul-ture of peeps like Jad use to make art, or to communicate in other ways, usually across very long distances. One tags one's design or message on an alley wall here in town, and someone whose imaging specs are tuned in from halfway around the world sees the tag pop up like old-school spraypaint on their bedroom wall, practically at the same time one is spraycasting it.

Jad's been a spraycaster just about long enough now that he's begun to discern different shades of meaning in the very texture of the spraystuff images he picks up.

It somehow always works out that Jad's hobbies have something to do with remote influence. Spraycasting's just the most recent, and the one he's pursued with the most resources. The greater the influ-ence exerted and the increasingly remote whatever the thing may be, the more beguiling it is to Jad. When he was a child, he'd designed kites that could navigate as high as the stratosphere and could shift between windborne and windless flight. A bit further on, by the time he'd put away about 1,500 school lunches, he'd worked as a student adjunct with an important geological survey on a project which compiled a glossary of vibratory "words" derived from data of periodic frequencies emitted from the planet's iron core, along with a syntax for the words, in order to "communicate" with the core. His favorite stories have always been those whose heroes operate from distinctive and idiosyncratic lairs, and whose incessant and fantastical adventures range from those lairs across the known continents and beyond. The foods he finds the most appetizing are those which are brought from across tectonic plates. Surprisingly, perhaps, Jad hasn't realized this thing about himself, this compulsion he has for remote influence, but he'll come to realize it yet. Maybe even in this story.

As Jad and Yenni look on, a Cubist caricature Jad's just drawn with the spraystuff gains a pictographic arrow through its head, drawn by an unseen hand from somewhere beyond. After a short pause, a goiter sprouts on the neck of the caricature, drawn as if yet a further insolent afterthought.

"Well, that's rude," Yenni remarks. Jad grins and throws his spraycan cap at the defiled drawing. The cap caroms off and lands near a set of bongo drums with a fist-sized hole punched through each head.

"Yeah, that's sort of the idea when you're first callsigning with another spraycaster somewhere. I suppose you could just add something to make a drawing better, but it's usually more fun this way. It's fun, at least, for one person at a time."

As Jad shakes his spraycan readying a reply, a spraystuff line begins to appear on some battered filing cabinets about a rubberband's-fling away. A picture forms.

"So, who is this person anyway?" Yenni asks. "Just someone you don't know somewhere you've never been who you already know you don't like?"

Jad gives her a sheepish sidelong glance. "You have a way of cutting to the quick of things, Yenni, don't you?" Jad starts ambling over to where the new drawing is taking shape. "I don't think I'm wasting your time, though. I didn't have you along just to help me find a great deal on mismatched footwear. In terms of directionality and backscatter and so on, the spraystuff seems to want to set up communication between specific delineated nodes. This junkyard and a specific other place, for example. Basically, having taken some readings and having picked up on cues from the person themself, I have very good reason to believe that this unmannerly spraycaster here is very close to Mispa's HomeHub. Whoever it is is probably tagging the HomeHub's porch steps right now. Maybe even the front door."

"You're kidding," Yenni says, stepping carefully over a puddle of viscous neon-blue runoff. "Are you sure?"

"These readings are pretty unassailable. I've been spraycasting back and forth with this person for a couple visits now. The HomeHub itself is physically intact, I'm sure, but it's been offline for decades. Completely out of commission. Interesting to have found it though, all the same. Based on where the tags are cropping up on their end, I've been able to model a rough map of the HomeHub with the, uh . . . raw materials."

"There're definitely plenty to-hand."

"Honestly, I really couldn't have asked for a better node than this junkyard. I've modeled the left front corner of the HomeHub with that vertical curtain rod over there, and the right front corner is this fence paling just here." Jad indicates the points with the nozzle-end of his spraycan. "The door's picked out by that red plastic sled I've stood up over there, and the floor of the foyer is marked by the linoleum squares laid out just beyond. It's like a mirage HomeHub, reflected from a point well past the horizon."

As Jad points out his markers, Yenni is actually able to begin visualizing the shape of the building which physically exists oceans away from this point, in a manner similar to that in which one envisions a fleshed-out image of a colossal tentacled mollusk or the metal-plated combatant who is destroyed by it, once the stars which make up the thing's constellation are identified. She absently dusts her hands off on her coveralls and wanders further along the perimeter of the skeletal structure.

Standing before the freshly-rendered filing cabinet tag now, Jad pauses and squints at the image. The unknown spraycaster has drawn a human figure with a life preserver around its waist. The figure has a perfectly square head with square eyes, and appears either to be in some sort of discomfort or is contorted in an attitude of mockery.

Within the context of spraycasting, an image which at first may appear juvenile, arbitrary, or vulgar may actually be tapping into a vernacular lexicon of pictograms and emblems with which other spraycasters are familiar and can respond to in a meaningful way. Jad smiles suddenly at the image, shakes his spraycan, and adds a triangle-shaped hat to the figure so that its head looks like a house. He draws a chimney on the house-hat, and trails a long wisp of smoke from it directly to where he reckons the threshold of the HomeHub is, there in that place where the birds sound nothing like they do here.

Now that he's verifiably onto something, it bears mentioning that Jad certainly hasn't selected this junkyard at random for his spraycasting node. What's more, and for no special reason, he hasn't been completely forthcoming about how he's come to have selected it. As it happens, Jad's descended from an ancestral line of some historical significance as it regards the type of work that he, Yenni, and hundreds of thousands of others perform at the top of their field . . . After all, *HomeHubs* were arguably the precursors to the TotalTongs of the sort we all recognize today, and may even have worked closely with at one point or another.

You see, Jad Filo's great-great-grandma, Mispa, was the revered houseringer of a stately HomeHub in the old country. The houseringer was something like Bond Barbian, or really just a topper in general. The role has evolved, of course, but the houseringer in those days when peeps hadn't given up on trying to make perpetual motion machines go, and when they had their hair textured in salons instead of just quickgrowing it the texture they wanted, was still the jar and gelatin of any grand manor with the retrofits, leveraging, and cultural buy-in required to call itself a HomeHub.

As a houseringer, Mispa wore the command jodhpurs. She had to make the chimney puff on cue. She had to be the mouthpiece and conscience behind any directive issued from the HomeHub. Mispa once had to euthanize the HomeHub's dog of seventeen years herself, with only a bottle of rubbing alcohol and a handkerchief. Perhaps most importantly, however, she had to believe at specific decisive moments that she could command a particular transcendental skill, even though she knew intellectually that this was impossible.

I could just about broast my dewlap right now, as I can't think of what the skill was called. It's not fashionable these days, not much talked about, and it was certainly discredited even by the time great-great-grandma Mispa was an established houseringer, but it was key in getting the HomeHub's retrofits to do what they needed to. Again, it was more to do with the houseringer's momentary belief that they could access the skill than it was the skill's real-world viability or scientificity. It was called something like "eggbeating" or "headspeaking" . . . Don't worry. It'll come to me.

Several weeks ago now, Jad had been perusing a bulletin board from a Glad Era archive he'd stumbled upon, which was stored on one of a bank of heirloom servers his family had stowed away in a data bungalow on the slate plains, at least a half-day's expedition from any metro area. Once he'd accessed the bulletin board and it had played him its theme song, Jad actually recalled hearing this music for the first time on a physical trip he took with his uncle when he was only half his mother's height, to the very data bungalow which hosted this server. One of the maintenance ghosts, it happened, had stopped transmitting after several decades with no previous interruption. For one reason or another, no one could raise it via picture-catching or spraycasting, and so his uncle had volunteered to investigate the problem on-site.

Jad had begged to be taken along. Though there was always an element of risk in an enterprise such as this, it was more than likely going to be a routine errand, and in the end it was just he and his uncle who made the trip. The upshot was that the maintenance ghost had sprung an extensor cam which prevented it from outstretching a stylus to the "ALL OK" button at the terminus of its rounds. Simple as that. The extensor cam's service life was rated at a hundred years, but these things happen. In a coup of inspiration, Jad's uncle replaced the cam with a whittled-down cartilage disk from the spine of a bison skeleton they'd spotted a few klicks from the bungalow.

When Jad punched up the heirloom server those few weeks ago, he found that it was the bulletin board's theme song he'd recalled from that trip above anything else. His uncle had routed the lifebits some years previous, but when Jad was a teenager, he received his uncle's account of what'd happened on the trip. Jad has no memory of his uncle's having talked their way past redundantly-armed sentries at a post about halfway along the route. He barely remembers the data bungalow itself. The bungalow's featureless from the outside, but it's a shade of purple that nothing in nature would ever be. It's a low-lying contoured shape that looks like the lid of a chafing dish, and it's about the size of a castle's cistern. On the slate plains, you can spot it while you're still an hour away.

The only means of physical access is a hydraulic platform in the center of the thing's roof. At the time he and his uncle had gone, it had been over fifty years since anyone had entered the data bungalow, and so the shell-like superstructure was full of those papery cubes parchment ants build as courting displays. Somehow parchment ants always find a way in. Jad has no memory of the server enclosure itself which might have seemed temple-like to him with its grid of blue-black prismatic columns containing dozens of blinking modules apiece. He's forgotten the looming maintenance ghost in its faintly luminous anti-static sackcloth covering and its conical hat it wears in order to connect to the power mains. The maintenance ghost glides from column to column fluttering wiry probes at one module or another, ticking and humming all the while. As he and his uncle were getting ready to leave, something Jad suspected was actual intentional music issued from an unlit sector of the server enclosure. The music didn't sound particularly mechanical, nor particularly organic. As Jad eventually found out, the music was rendered via a plectrum effect of "strumming" data needles and a woodwind effect of "reed buzzing" harmonic oscillators somewhere within the depths of a module. The server itself would have decided whether or not it was important to mike and packetize the sound for a remote user to hear.

"Why's that thing going off?" his uncle had grumbled. The beleaguered fellow traced the music, a music Jad had almost immediately recognized to be something like a "theme song", to Mispa's server, then decided it was nothing to concern himself over, and they'd made their exit and begun the return trip. A once-a-lifetime task, one Jad's parents and siblings would never have cause or inclination to undertake in all of their full natural lives, was completed without incident and Jad forgot all about it. Almost.

Stumbling onto Mispa's heirloom server those weeks ago from his apartment console, then, accessing the bulletin board and hearing the same theme song from all those years ago had led Jad quite the dance. He'd discovered a series of archived exchanges between Mispa and her beau, Kern, whose avatar in the exchanges was a crying cartoon cloud. That's all Jad knew about him as a person. Kern had immigrated here to Maldesia for work, and had settled not far from where Jad now lives.

Mispa was already a houseringer at that time, ensconced in her HomeHub and issuing directives to the neighborhood over which it presided, so she was staying put. Shortly after he'd arrived in Maldesia, Kern set up a spraycasting node in a meadow just outside town which yoked directly with Mispa's HomeHub back in the old country. All the technical information on the node was in the bulletin board archive. Kern's node was still active, of course, in the same spot it always had been since its setup. Now though, instead of a meadow it's a junkyard across whose scatterings of a generation's rubbish Jad and Yenni are currently picking their way.

Jad and the unknown spraycaster had exchanged another couple tags whose formally excellent cascade of pictographic aspersions and counter-jibes was endowing each of them with brick upon brick of street cred, at the same time it was getting Jad ever closer to completing his map of the HomeHub's street level.

Having cleared some irrelevant debris, Yenni helps Jad balance a broken foosball table on end, which stands in for where they've decided the electrical closet, and thus the fusebox, of the HomeHub must be. Jad shakes his spraycan and, directly in the center of the table, renders an anthropomorphic lightbulb flipping the caustic toast. He smirks and stands back. Almost immediately this time, a spraystuff hammer materializes above the lightbulb ready to smash it. The hammer handle twirls around the foosball table and ends in a stylized squiggle, the signoff tag of the remote spraycaster. End transmission.

"No, no, no! We were almost there!" In his frustration, Jad sprays a salvo of scribbles across the table. "Shit, Yenni, I'm going to have to keep coming back here till I can get this asshole on spraycast again!"

Yenni smiles mysteriously. "If I knew you were intending to reactivate this HomeHub, I might have an idea."

Jad looks momentarily stricken. "Reactivate it? What? I've got a good position as a nudger right here in Maldesia. Besides, a HomeHub is a completely different beast from a TotalTong. I'm no beast-whisperer."

"I'm not guessing at your motives," Yenni remarks. She wrinkles her forehead at him. "It sounds like you may be guessing at your own, though . . . It's just that I know you well enough to understand that any interest you may have in family history isn't going to motivate you by itself into wanting to climb over hillocks of stuff people have chucked out."

"Okay, yeah," Jad hits her companionably on the shoulder. "I was curious to see if I could jumper it. You hear stories about randos bringing defunct HomeHubs back online from across the sea, and it seemed plausible once I started working out a map for this one. You know as well as I do that spraystuff, apart from its obvious properties, can act as a conductor. If what's-their-face left their spraycan on auto, it'll complete the picture on their end, there at Mispa's HomeHub. That's how she exchanged messages with her guy over here, after all. I'm sure I just needed a couple more exchanges to be able to map the fusebox."

"Fine," Yenni says, pausing for a moment to see if Jad'll volunteer anything else. "So, I was going to say that it looks like your friend spraycasted right over the fusebox."

"What? Where?"

"Right there at the top. The hammer handle is rendered in a non-continuous line just there, and . . . there. Looks like something was in the way on their end."

Without another word, Jad plants a milk crate and stands atop it, spraying a series of fine parallel lines just at the point Yenni'd indicated.

Before long, something happens. Contours fill in of their own accord, and a roughly capsule-shaped image begins to take shape from several points at once. It's the HomeHub's fusebox automatically manifesting via its onboard spraycasting fixtures. With their imaging specs tuned in, Jad and Yenni look on. In about the time it takes for someone to call in a lunch order, a schoolbus-sized fusebox which is clearly for a different sort of system than those Jad is familiar with but which is still clearly a fusebox, is rendered in spraystuff on the foosball table and the surrounding debris in pristine geometric detail, mirroring a real-world object at the node on the other end.

"Yep," Yenni quips. "Looks like you jumpered it."

Jad stares slack-jawed.

"Wanna stop off at the depository on the way back to research the care and feeding of your new HomeHub?"

"Fuck." Jad squinches his eyes shut. "Now I'm gonna have to learn how to eggspeak."

He barely hears Yenni's laughter over the blood rushing in his ears, but he knows the laughter's at his expense.

{HEAVY EQUIPMENT:}

T he buildings here are all either more pointy or more rounded than the sorts of buildings peeps live in. The buildings are a lot bigger too, on average, though peeps have been living in bigger and bigger buildings. Why not have dinner with your business colleagues in the evening and work on closing the deal, and then have breakfast with your pandit in the morning and work on your spiritual development, after all? If you can do it all in the same building, even if it's from opposite corners of that building, you can leastwise use the same sewer system for everything. There's continuity in that. Family, in turn, materializes from continuity. Cornerstone of society and so forth, y'know? Anyhow, the pointiness and roundness of the buildings would suggest downtown to me . . . And now I can confirm it. Yep, we're downtown.

If I scoop you up with the gargoyles and radio masts, you'll see a colorful cordon of humanity wrapping itself around a couple city blocks over toward the south, lining up in a continuous slow-moving chain. It may seem like a particularly cruel form of punishment or a particularly stupid crowd control error, but it's just a fundraiser for a committee. The event's called Queueing for Queers.

The Queers are a political party whose platform is "algorithmic government" which attracts a lot of shiny-eyed young peeps these days, as well as a few oldsters who know what's what. The idea with the Queers is that if one is aware of the three biggest news stories in the capitol, the two biggest stories in the country, and the single biggest story across the globe, all of these Big Six officially broadcast by news consortium de rigueur Barrel Networks, the Big Six updated every four hours, then one can determine what sort of action the government will implement by following the branches down a standardized flow chart.

If nothing else, it's something to get riled up for and to blow off some steam about. Most activism accomplishes at least that much, and both the rile and the steam are vital to any political cause.

So, there's a part of this queue in particular which most peeps would notice. Let's Gleam In on it. Lucky for us, it'll serve our narrative continuity perfectly. Basically, it appears to be the chassis of one of those smaller front-loader tractors, and it's reminiscent of a single ski boot for a giant robot. The cab has been removed, and it's been replaced with a shower stall whose door has been welded shut. In fact, there are weld seams along all the vertices of this shower stall. The glass is flat and see-through, but the stall is filled to the top with a glutinous-looking gel. The gel is colorless, but because it's as thick as it is, it's as if the object inside is partly obscured by fog as seen from about a decameter away.

We can still see that it's Jad Filo in there, though, naked as a plucked eagle apart from a kind of skullcap chapleted with black knobs that look something like drawer-handles, and a minimalist breathing apparatus. He's floating mid-tank, waiting there in line inside this contrivance.

It's been a few weeks since that day in the junkyard when Jad reactivated Mispa's HomeHub, but a lot of peeps have already found out about it. Jad's TotalTong now knows, of course, so that's 500 right there. Jad's participating in this Queuing for Queers event with some colleagues from another tong too, known colloquially as "Mina Robards and the Mean Retards", so the word is spreading. The name of Mina's tong would've had to have been changed on account of its language, by the bye, but it isn't the actual name.

What Jad's having reactivated the HomeHub means in terms of protocol is that he's got first dibs at applying for the houseringer position. The job is government schedule, and starts out more than halfway up the chart, so it's well paid, but that's not why anyone would become a houseringer. For Jad (or anyone) getting the job would mean a lot of toil. For one thing, he'd have to help rebuild the neighborhood which's yoked under the HomeHub. For another, he'd have to onboard a helpstaff, get to know and to work with them sustainably, and establish his credibility. Apart from all those tasks which are understood to fall under the purview of houseringer, there are bound to be a steady supply of those "phantom tasks" that any houseringer can speak to. Mispa, for example, once had to rig an apparatus which equitably decided what to watch on TV any given evening, with only a wire hanger and an IR receiver yanked from a popcorn machine. A HomeHub, in addition to all the retrofits and the houseringer and helpstaff who do what they do "downstairs", is still a house tenanted by a nuclear family and is counted as a single-family house in the census.

Perhaps the most curious and taxing requirement for any would-be houseringer is that they must essentially trick theirself into believing they can eggspeak. Trickery is necessarily involved, as eggspeaking is a scientific impossibility. Successful eggspeaking would involve transmitting a signal along an avenue in which any detail is not permitted to exist. It would require being in control of a personal consciousness at the same time it would require abdication of every consciousness. Those who were supposed to have been capable of eggspeaking back in the Glad Era could impel the Widow Markowitz to perform a pirouette from across town simply by spinning a rolling pin in a dark closet. They could scratch strange verses on the inside surface of coconut rinds without cutting or opening the fruit. They could be simultaneously inside the hay barn and balancing atop the meetinghouse weathervane . . . You can almost see old chipped and worn decorative plates with these scenes cropping up at pawnshops while the world makes newer and more reliable ideas available to the entire population and cashes out their claim tickets, can't you?

In the hours and days after Jad reactivated the HomeHub, Yenni Mender and several others had helped get him set up for the training he'd need once he interviewed with the fusebox sometime within the next fiscal quarter, which was the standard deadline for making one's attempt at houseringer. Naturally, they'd begun by prepping him for the eggspeaking component. There's a well-established if somewhat obscure tradition of scholarship regarding the eggspeaking and houseringer connection, and Yenni herself had put Jad in touch with a couple of the peeps from Mina's tong, Riggs Neko and Fayban Rorch, who he happens to be queueing with now. The eccentric device they've helped him lash up is a fairly established blueprint for this sort of effort. Though this version is a shave more sophisticated, the same sort of thing has been built in the past with chariots and muslin, fish carts and a straw-filled suit of armor, and rollerskates and a wetsuit. The front-loader shower stall is, okay I'm gonna say it, a *pedagogical engine* which simulates the bodily dissociation aspects of eggspeaking. Let's call it an astral tractor. Basically, it's a mobile sensory-deprivation capsule, designed to produce the sensation of existing as a roving consciousness independent of a form. It's meant to model an impossibility in a plausible style.

Jad's the only one in line with anything approaching this setup, although someone else a couple parties ahead has one of those walking sticks that folds out into a seat. Everyone else appears to be on foot, queueing the normal way, so Jad's "footprint" is about ten times as big as anyone else's, and he takes up about two-thirds of the sidewalk width. Riggs and Fayban have helped Jad set up the astral tractor to keep to the streetside edge of the sidewalk wherever possible and to move forward at a constant rate of a kilometer an hour.

About fifteen-thousand peeps have turned out for the Queers today. The queue wraps around two city blocks, and most businesses along the way have their wares specially displayed out in front of their shops and geared to the event. The Queers attract a lot of TotalTong types, as their methods are similarly mechanistic. Honestly, about a quarter of those at the event belong to one tong or another. Riggs and Fayban, attending Jad, have exchanged greetings with about ten such peeps within shouting distance in either direction, and have spotted countless others beyond. Riggs has a buttery complexion, gestures with exaggerated movements, and is dressed completely in different shades of purple. Fayban's the one with overlong fingernails and underwear which is visible through his clothes.

"Is Jad's mic off?" Fayban asks.

"Yeah, he's in deepdive mode right now," Riggs responds, drawing hashmarks in the air. "He should be cycling around in about a half hour, and then we can check back in with him."

"I told him he could've accomplish this with crossed ankles," Fayban chirps. "It's probably how his, wotsit, his great-great-grandma prepped for it. No machine oil or acetylene torch necessary."

It was true. Houseringers of times past had known that exercises in bodily dissociation can begin most intuitively with crossed ankles. Keep your legs and feet still for several minutes and, if you're not looking or feeling, it becomes difficult to sense or to remember which ankle is crossed over the other. Mispa had used the technique when she was training, and continued to use it during her first stint as houseringer. She'd begin with the crossed ankles and then work her way up. Soon it didn't matter if she was looking at her ankles (and other elements of her already-dissociated anatomy) or not. By then, her eyeballs themselves had dissociated and were "showing" her something other than what she was looking at.

"Hey! Nice aquarium!" This from a pedestrian party traveling along the opposing sidewalk in a direction opposite the queue.

"Yeah, this is a rare specimen," Riggs calls. "He eats all the guppies we try to get him to tank-share with."

The party crosses over to the queuers to parley. Among them is a sixteen-year-old with a patently quickgrown coiffure, every individual hair kinked into the shape of square waves.

"You're in a TotalTong, yeah?" the square-hair grills.

"Yep," Riggs grins. "7YRE52. We're a manufacturing outfit here in the city. I'm a hedger. Fayban here's a stropper."

"You guys are Mean Retards?"

"Wow," Fayban blurts, honestly surprised. "How'd you know our handle? Just from the alphanumeric?"

"It's my sister. She's a bringer, so she knows most of the tongs that operate in this area."

"Yeah," interrupts another of the interloping party, this one all of fifteen years with clothes made entirely from sofa upholstery. "We heard from her about *this* guy," sofa-clothes says, giving the side of Jad's shower stall a resounding thwack before anyone has a chance to counsel against it. Still, Jad appears to be oblivious to them. "So he's, what, going to . . . *whittle* a relay? By himself?"

"Hmmm, pretty apt actually," Fayban remarks, advancing a half-step in line.

"Yes," Riggs pronounces. "From your sister, then, you know that most modern companies, and any that a TotalTong work with, have both a fusebox and a proprietary relay. The fusebox is a big calculator that holds a current copy of all the critical company data, and inside the fusebox is the relay which is basically a mechanical program that runs on it."

"We've seen that stuff too," square-hair jabbers. "The fusebox where my Da works is the size of an old locomotive boiler. He's a technician. There's a little window in the fusebox where you can see the relay spinning and jittering in there."

"Right, right," Riggs continues. "So you probably also know how TotalTongs approach work with a new company. The topper and a few others from the tong meet with the company, encode the company's position as it currently stands, and take a full audit of the fusebox's configuration. While doing the work we do, the tong either uses the company's actual fusebox or a working mock-up.

We begin with a brand new relay, smooth on every surface, no data whatsoever, and we inscribe it. That is the work of a TotalTong, plain and simple. Inscription. It takes all 500 of us, each one a specialist in a discrete aspect of the business, working one to a few weeks, depending, each of us making precise manual adjustments to the fusebox as we go, usually scores of us at the same time. Finally, out comes the relay, etched to perfection. Usually, a relay's good for a fiscal quarter before it has to be redone, but some outfits change them out monthly. Really special jobs, say at a pivotal make-it-break-it time for a company, may produce a relay that's designed with very specific results in mind which's only good for a few days to a week."

Square-hair's eyes have glazed over, but sofa-clothes musters "A relay I once saw, freshly installed in a fusebox, looked like a wasp's nest as big as a saloon piano."

"I'd like to think the relays we finish with look more like candy-floss as big as a band organ," Fayban cracks.

"So, then," Riggs plows on, "You understand the challenge Jad here intends to undertake. Though the equipment looks different, though the models may vary, TotalTongs and HomeHubs use the same technology, fuseboxes and relays, to achieve a similarly complex success. Hopefully.

In our case, the TotalTong, we aim for the growth and general success of a business. With the HomeHub, the aim is the development and prosperity of a residential neighborhood."

"And this shower thing on a tractor's going to help?" Square-hair chews her lip skeptically.

"Riggs and I didn't think this thing up on our own," Fayban remarks. "The astral tractor's been in use for decades now. Decades at least. It enables a pilot to move through an environment while selectively muting most sense cues. That's a topical anesthetic gel Jad's immersed in in there which also diminishes his hearing and smelling right down to baseline. Believe it or not, he can still see almost normally.

The backstory here is that houseringers interface with their fuseboxes more directly than anyone in a TotalTong does; even a topper. Not only does a houseringer inscribe their relay singlehandedly, they establish a feedback loop with the fusebox as they do so, and are guided by it along the way. When Jad has his interview with the HomeHub fusebox, he's going to wear a hat much like the one he's got on in here." Fayban nods toward Jad's contrivance inching along on its continuous tracks.

"Yep, that cap's covered in electrodes and will be interfaced with the fusebox," Riggs adds. "It just so happens that a HomeHub fusebox favors a physiological state in which a person thinks they're egg-speaking, at least while the relay's being etched. The houseringer does all the etching by hand too, with completely manual tools. Not like us folks in TotalTongs do, depressing flippers and pulling toggles on a fusebox mock-up while the relay slowly rotates and wobbles inside. Of course, eggspeaking's impossible and Jad's 'boffin brain' knows this. The astral tractor's a convincing sim of one aspect of eggspeaking, though. It's training wheels, is what it is. Back in the Glad Era, a houseringer would go into trance to manage all this. Today, we've got, well . . . ready access to machine oil and acetylene torches." Riggs jabs Fayban in the ribs.

The day's been wearing on now, and the curious interlopers have long since abandoned the scene. Jad, flanked by Fayban and Riggs up until the 03:00 Gray Line run some time ago now, is once again level with the event booth which marks both the end and the beginning of the queue. Here, the Queueing for Queers event staff would hoot, throw prizes, and garland participants with plastic necklaces.

Fayban and Riggs completed three circuits of the queue in about as many hours before going home, or going to wait in an actual queue for dinner, or whatever it was they did. At that time, there were only a couple thousand participants remaining.

Now though, the sun's a molten dome on the horizon. No one from the event remains, save Jad. He'll probably go the circuit once more until his pals return and de-slosh him. Until then, Jad'll be anywhere his conspiring neurons whisper him to. This afternoon alone, he's been lining up for a ride down a waterslide off the edge of the world with a multitude of teardrop-shaped monopods, he's been part of a slow-moving procession of a myriad leathery simians through an arcane wick-lit city made entirely of paraffin, and he's joined a solemn cavalcade of fifteen-thousand gaunt fusiliers each dressed in ridiculous dimestore-style arthropod costumes (lobsters, trilobites, butterflies, centipedes, and tarantulas, all) plodding off toward the deepest sector of a trombone-colored desert.

Mispa's fusebox would be impressed, wouldn't it?

I'm assuming both of you want the Jim? Scoop of butter pecan, then a scoop of raspberry ripple, and pistachio on top?" The man behind the counter dips his scooper into a hot-water well and pauses expectantly.

"What tipped you off, Sal?" Yenni Mender inquires. "Was it the lifeless gaze or the bad haircut? Yeah, we'll each have one."

Sal smiles, and scoops a Jim for Yenni, and one for Fayban Rorch. Both of them take a single lick of their cone, and then thank Sal and walk outside.

The way the clouds are stacked today makes the roadway look grayer than usual. There are three wrought iron café chairs lined up by the plate glass windows in front of Sal's. Each chair has a rosebush design that digs uncomfortably into your back whenever you sit in it. A familiar-looking man walks past and makes a clasped-hands signal to them. Yenni raises her ice cream cone to him in a subtle gesture.

"That guy's a . . . dregger, isn't he? Is he with Rita's tong? I think I met him at a social dance a couple quarters ago."

"Yeah, he's a dregger," Fayban pronounces, "I think he's with Immington's outfit, actually. They're a marine cargo tong."

"Chris Immington and the Christian Indians?"

"That's them . . . Okay, are we gonna do this?" Fayban is already tilting his cone so that the ice cream scoops are precariously sliding across each other.

"That's what we're here for."

As if it were a choreographed action, Yenni and Fayban tip their cones just enough so that the scoops fall off and plop onto the edge of the sidewalk. Six forlorn globes of ice cream, arrayed like the impacts on a crater field, begin to melt into the gutter. This path the pair are tramping, the Way of Jim, started as a joke but it's become a thing of some earnestness, or maybe it's the other way around.

Yenni started it, or Jad or Riggs did, but now dozens of TotalTong peeps participate in tramping the Way. Jim was a retail clerk, maybe totally made up, or maybe a synthesis of a few such figures. One day Jim was split up with at a fast food restaurant, discovered his car had been booted at a mini golf parking lot, unwittingly dropped his cone in front of an ice cream parlour, and finally theatrically quit his job at a makeup store in order to take back his life via a newfound sense of agency. Jim's is a story of resistance against one's prevailing loserdom, and acceptance of the subsequent tolerable situation one stumbles into from there. Tramping the Way involves following Jim's route of that fateful day, visiting his four stops in order (four existing places on the map) and performing a symbolic devotional at each stop.

Having completed their dropped-cone devotional, Yenni and Fayban proceed down the sidewalk in the direction of Cosmologie, the Grent Road location of the makeup franchise where Jim tendered his resignation.

The news of the moment, likely to be the news of the next several weeks, is Jad's successful interview at the HomeHub. It's been almost two months since the day he was Queueing for Queers in his astral tractor. Apparently the interim effort has paid off. Yenni had seen Jad off three days ago by sea train. It had taken a full day's travel there, to the land where Mispa had long ago plied her craft. Jad had reported to the HomeHub as soon as he'd arrived, but the fusebox had denied him interview and had physically locked him out until the next day. The interview itself, once it had commenced, had lasted the better part of a day; morning and night. Naturally, Jad was fitted with his electrode skullcap the whole while. He hardly spoke a word. Most of the assessment was done using neurofeedback, and an array of other biofeedbacks at the same time. Part of the interview consisted of Jad's handworking a model relay about the size of a cat carrier. When the relay was run against a simulation, it had miscalculated the neighborhood's natural gas requirements for the month by about the amount that would fill a dirigible, and had successfully contained about half the second-alarm fires, but in the end Jad had passed the interview and had accepted the houseringer position then and there.

He'd sent Yenni some snaps of his electrode-embossed scalp and the inscribed model relay via picture-catching this morning along with a telegrammatic version of the news. Yenni'd reached out to Fayban, and the two decided to do a "Jim" pilgrimage and catch each other up on everything.

"So," Yenni begins, "Are you surprised he did it?"

"I didn't think he had a chance, honestly. Not until a day or so before he left, and then I was sure he *would* succeed. It makes me think we've been going at it all wrong. Like, for anyone who's trying to qualify as a houseringer."

"How do you mean?" Yenni asks, skirting a patch of wet cement. "You don't think the shower stall on tank treads is what cinched it for him?"

"That's all part of the traditional prep," Fayban singsongs. "I'm talking systemically here. I don't think Jad has ever believed he can eggspeak; not even momentarily. I don't think he believed it at any moment while he was doing his interview yesterday."

"Isn't eggspeaking the cornerstone of what he's meant to do?"

"It *was*, or it *should* have been. That was the idea we were trying to instill these last months. I think Jad discovered another way of getting the feedback the fusebox is looking for. I think he intuited it just a few days ago."

"He never mentioned anything to you about not needing to eggspeak?"

"No. I was paying close attention though. Especially toward the end. We'd start with dialectics, do some exercises in muscle memory, and then go from there. The work was conforming to a level I'd have expected, but then it seemed like Jad was humoring me as we went on. I caught him out a couple times toward the very end."

The pair round the corner onto Grent Road, following the Way of Jim. Now the sign for Cosmologie is just in view on the next block up.

"Try one on me, one of those dialectic spiels. I'm curious. Vis-à-vis eggspseaking, I mean."

"Yeah?" Fayban smiles bashfully and pauses. "Okay, then. A typical one might go something like this: 'Try walking a dog. Okay? Now try walking a bird. Alright? Now try walking the moon. Your consciousness shifts as a dog you're walking sniffs a tree, as a bird you're walking builds a nest, as the moon you're walking shines on someone halfway around the world from you. It effectively extends your consciousness.'" Fayban glances over at her with hooded eyes. "Okay, so now you respond. Do so the way you would in a conversation with . . . yourself."

Yenni smirks. "The moon doesn't walk."

"Okay. Don't worry about that. Figure of speech. The moon travels as you're paying attention to it, as you're also traveling."

"So, the premise is that walking the moon extends my consciousness. What if what it really does is *commandeers* my consciousness?"

"Sure, in an ever-expanding array, from one commandeering pilot, to another, to another. That's just another way of calling it what it's meant to be."

"Yeah, but these remote tendrils, dogs, birds, and moons, aren't tandem supplements to our own consciousness. They're disconnected from our native senses, our knowledge base, and our thought processes."

Fayban gives her a look like "This could go on for some time," and Yenni comically shrugs her shoulders.

"So Jad and I would go through about a half-hour of dialectics like that, and then he'd put on the electrodes. I'd coach him through some mudras and other hand-gesturey muscle memory things while we monitored the neurofeedback. At some previous time, I'd accidentally mapped a couple electrode sites incorrectly on the readout. I'd flip-flopped them. Still, the readout was consistent with how it ought to have looked if I'd mapped them correctly. I didn't discover my mistake till later."

"So . . . ?"

"So it was as if one section of his brain instantly did what another section was expected to do, and vice versa. Almost as if to keep up appearances with the readout. It would be like ordering Swiss cheese on your sandwich, and the order taker accidentally punches cheddar on his console. Meanwhile, the console sees what's about to happen, and momentarily rewires the Swiss and cheddar buttons so that the order is fulfilled as expected. The order taker is none the wiser. I purposely repeated this flip-flop a couple times over the next few weeks and got the same result."

"Wow. Maybe Jad really can eggspeak."

Fayban chuffs a laugh. "Conversational Latin would be more useful, I think."

Cosmologie is now only about a lawn dart's throw away and a couple other pilgrims have just emerged from the place and are doing hamstring stretches on the sidewalk out front.

"I'm still trying to get my head around how Jad's going to manage inscribing a relay with so spare a workforce," Yenni reflects. "As I understand, he'll have a helpstaff, his technical crew. Still, they really don't amount to much."

"Usually about five altogether," Fayban affirms. "What's more, the helpstaff don't have anything to do with physically inscribing the relay."

"I don't know. Part of what made me want to be in a TotalTong is that you're operating at such an enormous scale. When I was a kid, my Da took me along on a day when his tong was inscribing a weeklong relay. They were working in a hangar out on the slate plains. The relay was installed in a mock-up fusebox about as tall as a jet airplane, and it was covered as if by a fishing net with people in the tong. There were maybe a hundred people outside the hangar waiting to sub in at their critical moment, but the balance of the tong, hundreds, were all working on the inscription at once. Fifty or more people were on top of the fusebox, and the rest were arrayed all around, some standing on chairs or stepladders, others on sections of scaffolding which had been erected.

I stood next to my Da, a lamper, who watched, listened, sniffed, and only moved his small part of the fusebox whenever his expertise dictated. The impression of all those hundreds of people performing their single specialty, depressing flippers, pulling toggles, dialing gauges, all of them doing so in that circumscribed area, had a powerful effect on me. It was like being inside a planet when it's first starting to form, like the needle-tip ignition of an explosion as big as the world. It was a powerful and electrifying thing.

I've never experienced an impulse of wanting to pare that down."

"I think anyone in a TotalTong has felt that way. There's the joke about it being like an army tying a shoelace, but the joke completely misses the point. Divide shoelace-tying into 500 discrete steps, and parcel each out to a specialist in that step. The resulting shoelace will be unerringly tied to the rigorous specification your organization requires, every time."

"And now I'm ready to spec out this pilgrimage . . . You ready?"

"Let's do it!"

Without further delay, Yenni and Fayban each sweep open a door of Cosmologie and march up to the front counter. A buffed and spangled cosmetologist stifles a pat greeting in his throat once he recognizes the two. It takes the pair all of ten seconds to grab a lipstick tube in each hand and to render derisive spectacles and mustaches on their faces, to draw in angry forehead lines with eyebrow pencils, and to rouge up some livid outrage on their cheeks, just as Jim did on the day he took back his life, all to the whoops and eggings-on of staff and patrons alike.

{HUMAN RESOURCES:}

I'm always struck by the way the sky blends with the trees here. Back in Maldesia, the mingling of trees and sky is reminiscent of nothing so much as a button-down shirt and necktie hovering everywhere, partway up the heavens. Here, the colors and forms of the tree-sky margin are never so staid, even as they're pruned and smogged by modern development. Here, these garret-level elements combine in indelicate fandangos and in sudden vigorous skirmishes, often laying low both reticence and good sense alike.

The buildings, lamps, bus stations, and street grates are similarly undomesticated. Their skins are brightly colored, hand rendered, and imaginatively repaired.

Yenni's here, and it appears she's only visiting, as she's carrying a portmanteau and is glancing about as if trying to spot a landmark or to check a streetsign. She's wearing her customary coveralls, though she looks particularly well-turned-out in these ones. The coveralls are clearly bespoke, they're crafted from the best material in the season's colors, and pinned to them is a gleaming badge that she hasn't worn for very long.

I may as well tell you she's moved the long way from Maldesia a few short months ago. Her work is based in the city some two hours or thereabouts from here, but she's never actually seen a phase-three neighborhood under the jurisdiction of a HomeHub before, there still aren't any HomeHubs in Maldesia after all, and this is one such neighborhood.

As far as *this* phase-three neighborhood goes, it really does appear to have benefitted from the HomeHub system, especially compared to the surrounding sun-cracked and somewhat lackadaisical boroughs she's traveled through on her way here. For example, she's just passed a fruit cart in which none of the fruit is spoiled, and on whose sideboard is no trace of the disreputable broadsheets she's seen on other such carts in other places. Everyone is moving about energetically, though never frantically. Altogether, the place seems a bastion of civic vigor and good taste.

Her work is fundamentally the same as it has been for the last thirty-odd years. Along with her TotalTong, it's the inscribing of a relay which accounts for the sequence of augmentations, diminishings, emphases, deemphases, accelerations, and decelerations which will empower a client to meet their organizational goals, all of it evaluated on 500 factors which are all in flux. Of course, twenty years on from that day Jad officially immigrated from Maldesia, Yenni hasn't been idle. She's bootstrapped herself from humble flagger to a job title which certainly has a better ring to it.

Passing a pristine bicycle rack, Yenni comes level with an alleyway and has another unobstructed view of the HomeHub itself. It is literally on a hill, and looks like a cross between a residential house, a power plant, and a factory. It's sided as a house is, and is even gabled with several casement windows on the compact upper stories, but the base of the building is as thick around as a battleship. The smokestack is made to look like a brick chimney, and it's presently liberating a pall of gossamer effluvium which hangs in the air and describes abstract pinwheels and propellers there before it slowly disperses. There are four supply pipelines as wide as gazebos issuing from each side of the HomeHub, trailing off into different sections of the neighborhood. The whole edifice is painted a lurid shade of "caution orange", but this is per regulation as Yenni understands.

A car horn close by arrests her attention, and in the direction she turns to look, she sees a large stucco building with a colorful awning under which a lone person stands reading a book. Something familiar about the person makes her double-take, and then she finds herself actually moving across the street in the direction of the person. Her feet have already confirmed who it is that her eyes believe she's recognized . . . Surgeons on sedatives! Would you believe it's Jad Filo? What're the odds?

Jad blinks when he sees Yenni. He blinks again, and then cracks a huge smile as she closes the gap between them to allow the spontaneous hug to happen.

"Jad! I can't believe I just ran into you like this! I was sure I'd have to ping the HomeHub."

"Oh," Jad chuckles nervously, "Don't worry about that."

"No? Well, I'm obviously glad I encountered you out, you know, just out and about." Yenni squints at his book whose cover is flashing: ABRIDGED EDITION . . . CONTACT PUBLISHER FOR MISSING ILLUSTRATIONS. "What're you reading?"

Jad looks at the book as if he's forgotten about it. "Oh yeah, these are annoying, these books that switch? In the store, this one had a cover blurb about a giant map inside. The dust jacket had something about the edition being fully annotated and unexpurgated, so I bought it and was about three blocks away before the cover changed to admit the book wasn't that special after all. This is about the third time I've gotten burnt like this.

Forget about that, though. I haven't seen you in, what, fifteen years? What brings you out here?"

"I think it's closer to twenty, actually. Last time I visited, you were still just getting started. I was going to let you know I was here, honest. I've only arrived a few days ago, and I was excited to see the developed neighborhood."

"So you're here for a visit?"

"Can you believe I live here now? Well not *here* here, obviously, but a couple hours away in the city." Yenni unconsciously touches her badge.

"Whoa!" Jad's face unfurls. "You're a topper!"

Yenni gives a short laugh "Well yeah. I, um, my tong here is known as Yenni Mender and the Yuppie Mariners. You know how TotalTongs have taken off here in the last year or two. I took an opportunity. I really have been meaning to reach out to you, Jad."

"No, I mean I didn't hesitate to pull up stakes when the HomeHub thing came up for me. I understand how stuff happens so fast."

"Yeah," Yenni picks up her portmanteau and sets it back down. "It's probably rude of me to ask, not having talked with you in so long, but how ever *did* you appear to be eggspeaking, anyway? You know, when you were training with the guys back home, and then when you interviewed? You must still do it regularly enough, even now, while you're inscribing relays."

Jad looks surprised. "Wow. I'd have thought I'd told you already . . . I just visualized myself spraycasting the relevant parts of the fusebox as if I were still in the junkyard, using my model there. It was much more intuitive to me. Besides, it would apply a sort of physical displacement effect, just as that one aspect of eggspeaking was supposed to have done." Jad tosses his book into a nearby trash can.

"Honestly," he continues, "It was much better than those exasperating dialectics, at least for me. There are only so many times you can have 'conversations with yourself' about how when one of our species was on the moon it stretched humanity's telepathic thread further that it'd ever been stretched, or how if everyone in the world was crammed into the same country we'd all know each other's favorite color without having to ask."

Yenni pulls a face. "I'd had about enough after the first statement Fayban Rorch gave me as an example. In any case, that's great, Jad. You're as talented as the best of them. The neighborhood looks great!"

They both wince as a loudspeaker mounted under the awning buzzes in a too-loud modulation, "Number 103, please. 103."

"Okay, Yenni," Jad says, glancing at a ticket in his hand. "I've got to go, but I'm really glad we ran into each other like this. Good luck to you."

"Of course!" Yenni says, exchanging another hug with him. "Now I'm here, we ought to meet up sometime soon and catch up."

"We'll do it!"

With that, the two separate and Jad recedes behind a set of opaque doors. The traffic on the streets and sidewalks is as energetic as ever. If Yenni's noticed the text on the awning, she hasn't let on. The awning reads "Employment Agency".

CAREER PATH

L eft turn.
Left turn.
Right turn here at the sharply-branching "Y".

Corn grows in about twenty types of soil, but only in about three types of climate. There's a lesson there somewhere, Keff's sure. Whether it means she can be less painstaking about some things or that she has to specialize more, she's less than sure. These days, she supposes she can stand to benefit from either of those.

Left turn.
Right turn.
Straight on at the three-way.

What Keff's always appreciated is how the corn ramparts in these builds interact with the horizon at each turn. If you keep your head perfectly straight, the axis of your body in line with the path, and you walk along the path's middle at a steady rate, you can keep track of how many times and at what frequency you see those certain landmarks which are taller than the corn. You can work your way out that way alone. That's Nonny's favorite method of quickly remembering the solution to a corn maze like this one. Leave it to Nonny to solve one problem with the solution to another she finds more interesting. Keff wonders if Nonny's finished with her errands today and if she'll be able to meet up for coffee later.

Right turn.
Left turn.
Another left here at an incurving wall.

"Hey, Keff," says a voice which she imagines a baboon speaking in. "Haven't we been this way already? I think I recognize these stalks." A titter of collective laughter follows.

"No, really," the voice continues. "There're those big tassels on top, and the ears kind of spiral around the stalks like those old-fashioned hat racks at Ridley's department store."

It's Faz who's spoken. Keff's sure it's Faz because of the voice, of course, but also because of the misbuttoned buttons on his shirt.

"Honestly, Faz," she says, "At this stage, the point is not to arrive at the most elegant solution to the corn maze. It's just to get the hell out. At all. If we get out at the opposite end from where we started, so much the better."

Keff Stewart is leading a classroom-size group of people through a sixty-acre corn maze which is a quarter-scale reconstruction of a 200-year-old corn maze from the classical heyday of corn mazes. Faz is actually one of her favorites from this group. She'll never let on though, even if it could be considered ethical, which it can't. Faz has good intuitions about why people do the things they do, she thinks, and he reveals these intuitions in consistently amusing fashion. He's total crap at mazes, though.

Another few twists and Nyl speaks up. Nyl's really not at the right place to make a career or even a hobby out of this, and Keff suspects she's been coming along on these "assays" simply to avoid other shadowy unpleasantries in her life which have been hinted at but not laid bare. "I'm not sure about you guys," Nyl says, "But I'm going to need an hour or two at the Steam Room after this."

The Steam Room is a bar where everyone wears only white towels. There is no actual steam. Keff's fairly certain that Nyl has never been to this bar, though it's probably about the fourth week she's mentioned needing to go. For one thing, no one has expressed an interest in going with her. For another, Nyl is a textbook self-abnegator. Keff actually pictures Nyl now as an alligator pettishly thrashing a side of beef away from herself with a powerful swing of her tail.

"Okay," Keff says, absently scratching at her chin with the tines of a dinner fork she's clutching. "We're exactly halfway through the corn maze. I'll give you guys that freebie. At this point, assuming we're taking the correct path, we're one left turn up on right turns. The next junction's a two-way. Is it left or right that's going to be the next turn along the correct path?"

"Ummm," this is Heston. Keff can tell from the exaggerated gesticulations accompanying monosyllabic utterances. "Is it left?"

"Interesting answer," Keff replies, twirling her fork. "Statistically, you'd be correct. Another left would be a perfect throw-off, wouldn't it? Think of the society that built this corn maze, though. This was directly after Heldig Minks left office, during the interregnum."

"Oh. Yeah. It's got to be right, then." An explosion of laughter erupts from those closest by.

"Yep." Keff makes the right turn and the group follow. "The Flittsburgites were obsessed with parity at this point. Every political party had to have the same representation as all the others. State-run organizations were very regimented and standardized. All that ideology trickled down into the culture, even as far as it came to aesthetic intent. The designer of this corn maze, Yeskar Band, was herself an elected Bumbly."

Keff takes out her phone and styluses through a few screens with the rubber butt-end of the fork.

"Yeah," she continues, "I mean, this stuff isn't a science in the test tubes and slide rulers sense, but it can be approached that way. That's all I'm really trying to get across here."

Keff's a trained sociologist. She did her grad work in maritime sociology. These days, she's switched her focus to terrestrial sociology; corn mazes in particular, as they relate to the societies that create them. Something like that's her official mission statement, anyway. Honestly, she's lost focus on why it is that people make mazes, and why they make them the way they do. More and more, she's generally convinced that none of the "Five W's" are the right question. Besides all that, she really believes she's doing better sociology simply by brute-forcing the solution out of a freshly-furrowed maze. The implication, from the dawn of humankind to last Tuesday, is that mazes are meant to be assayed *bodily*. Not in some namby-pamby newsstand puzzle book.

Also, Keff is seven months pregnant. From the moment she'd found out, she'd decided that the only serious relationship she has time or inclination for anymore is the relationship with her currently-gestating progeny.

Her pregnancy's dovetailed in a way with her philosophical crisis over terrestrial sociology (or aesthetic crisis, or pedagogical crisis, or whatever it may be considered by a licensed crisis expert). Since then, she's had about a dozen moments of lucidity a week in which she sees the entire industry in a farcical light. This, either in spite of or because of the fact that she herself has devoted years to the study's research, explication, and codification.

Of course, intangible legacies like these have a nasty habit of making even their closest adherents feel just this way from time to time. Unless whatever it is you're doing is correlated to a moonbound rocket, an assembly line, or the advent of a cheaply-manufactured line of high-performance footwear, you're going to doubt yourself and be doubted by others. Keff was well aware of this effect as well.

Seven months ago now, Keff had been invited to speak on a panel at a terrestrial sociology conference organized by that bastion of learning and repute, Ack Tarminy. She'd been comped all expenses for the entire conference, and had only left her hotel room for the first two days to purchase some safety razors and a couple postcards. The third day was the panel on which she was to appear, so she went along to the conference which was being held at the big downtown convention center there.

Keff's intentions were good. She sat through the first half hour of a talk on subconscious intent in rock garden design, and then went to the restroom where she camped out in a stall dawdling on her phone for about another half hour. The whole time, though she couldn't make out what was being said, the low frequencies of the amplified speech reached her there in the restroom stall. The sound was hypnotic, and she was sure if she returned to her seat that she'd fall asleep within the first few minutes and probably end up snore-drooling. Not exactly the impression she cared to instill with colleagues.

Keff exited the restroom. As she wandered over toward concessions, she was struck by the design elements of the convention center, and so she wandered a little more. The building was about a hundred years old, and some of the original design elements either still appeared or were echoed here and there in different parts of the structure.

Keff had started exploring at the top level of the building. She'd happened to have learned that this floor had been added only a few years ago, and so any elements it may have shared with the original building design would have been imitative. A polyresin-topped informational placard drew her attention to the bitumen-colored entablatures which were an apparent reference to the center's most recent cash infusion having originated from a benefactor who ran a nearby refinery, but the building itself made her notice the *scepter* motif which recurred every couple meters along the cornices.

The scepter, whenever it occurred, was quite detailed. Depicted in molded relief was the gourd-shaped finial and the individual jewels of that most-recognized bauble of sovereign office. She followed examples of the scepter motif down a lavish curving stairway which opened onto another large hall from which the mid-tier seats of the auditorium could be accessed. There, she came up short as she recognized the chair of terrestrial sociology from an affiliate university by his distinctive garb, barely a lawn dart's throw away at the other end of the hall. This was the fellow who'd sponsored her for the conference and who may have already tried unsuccessfully to contact her a few times since the conference's start some two-plus days ago. Keff may have set incoming calls to go straight to voicemail. He was on the phone looking distracted, leafing through what appeared to be a conference program. There were less than ten milling people in the hall altogether, the conference was mid-talk after all, but he hadn't spotted her.

This was her one chance for redemption. She could rush over to him, make any sort of half-convincing excuse, and everything would have gone on the way it had. No one would have had cause for embarrassment, and her career would have gone unbesmirched. The first thing she became aware of once again at that moment, however, was the droning sound coming over the public address of whomever it was speaking at the moment. Rashaal Wettucks, from the sound of it. Keff shuddered and escaped along a side passageway.

Here, along corridors which accessed coatrooms, display cases, and other amenities, the motif continued. Something like it did, anyway. Keff had assumed these were more scepters until she paid attention. The designs in relief along this floor were *maces* of the kind used to settle disputes in the times of stone and iron. In other words, the motifs now depicted rodlike implements for bashing someone's head in. The mace was as detailed as the scepter. The spheroidal business end of the thing was festooned with pointed knobs, and there was a stretched-leather grip at the base, presumably to ensure no-slip grappling.

This level of the convention center had been added on some fifty years ago. Keff wondered if the scepters that were rendered decades later along with the entire level above were simply a misread of the mace, or if this was a conscious softening-of-edges from weapon to ornament-of-office. Of course, she reflected, the scepter of sovereign rule had often served up only a more genteel form of head-bashing, administering the blow to certain classes and races steadily and methodically over the course of human lifetimes rather than at the speed of a muscle-contraction on a battlefield.

Smiling a bit at her own high-flown analysis, Keff descended another stairway, strolled another level of the center, and continued to pick out other iterations of the ball-and-stick motif along the way. Finally, following her logical progress to its inevitable terminus, Keff made her way down to the basement. This was the hundred-year-old foundation of the place, and it showed.

The first clue that conference-goers weren't intended to venture down to this foundational level were the exposed electrical panels in various places along the walls, and the condensation-dripping pipes above them. The lighting was dim and sparse, and various items which had been taken out of service such as carpets, fixtures, and seating were stacked willy-nilly along the walls. Behind the newer electrical and data lines, however, remained what was surely the original structure. The glazed brick walls here were generally grimy and ill cared for, but as Keff peered at another stretch of exposed mold-ing, she laughed aloud. The motif depicted here in plaster relief was, in actual fact, a flax plant.

It was unmistakable. Represented were the segmented boll sitting bulbously atop a spindly stem, the carpels coming to a gentle point like the onion dome of an Orthodox praisehouse, and the fish-teeth petals bolstering the whole affair. A flax plant through and through. To think that architects of the next hundred years would have looked at the original design drawings and seen these motifs as manmade objects of rule and conquest was all too symptomatic of the vainglorious human race. All of it would have been the making of a terrestrial sociology thesis project in itself.

Keff followed the flax motifs down another hallway to where they seemed to converge on a highly ornamented lintel and pair of jambs to a door with a light coming from under it. Taped to the door was a handwritten sign which read "STAFF BREAKROOM". Keff knocked tentatively, and then, having received an answering hello, haltingly opened the door.

There was a man in the room bent over a low table which was like a wide and shallow box with an open top. He was rooting through an assortment of pom-poms, short lengths of yarn, mylar tassels, and small plastic doodads. A sensory table is what these things are called, Keff thought. The man looked up distractedly from the table and greeted her by name.

His face was blurred, as was the name on his conference ID badge. If for some reason he'd had his federal scan-fob, birth certificate, or medical records along, those would've been blurred too, just as anyone's would have been to her since the incident about three years ago now, but Keff could never mistake her old classmate, Bren Hargus.

Keff and Bren had always enjoyed an ambiguous association with each other. They'd been in the same undergrad program, and now Bren was avoiding this conference in a similar present-but-unaccounted-for manner, much the same as Keff was.

Thinking back, Keff still can't account for how catching up with a colleague like Bren for a couple hours while mutually rummaging around in a sensory table might have lead to sharing one of the most intimate of human acts, second only to the pelvic exam, especially having done so on a pile of rolled up carpet runners pushed to the side of the room, but share she had.

What's more, the thing that concluded their romp was only a prolonged silence. A speaker in the ceiling of the room had been softly broadcasting the audio of the conference the whole time. It had been easy to ignore up to that point, but then it dawned on Keff all at once that her panel was well underway, and that there was a pause as her name was announced and she was not, in fact, approaching the lectern from the wings. Obviously, she was in a staff breakroom a couple floors below the seats-20,000 auditorium in her underwear. After almost a full two minutes of silence, the announcer clumsily apologized for Keff's absence and ushered on the next part of the panel. At that point, whatever spell that may have been at work keeping her there for as long as it had was magically broken. There wasn't much else for her to do than to tell Bren how nice it had been catching up, to awkwardly scrabble into her clothes, and to catch the cab that would take her away from the convention center quicker than any of the others.

There was an envelope waiting for her at the front desk when she returned to the hotel some hours later. It was a ticket home, and with it was a terse letter explaining that her original return ticket had been cancelled, along with the remainder of her hotel stay. Keff thought this was a somewhat petty manner of blackballing her, but blackballed she'd been. This became clear in the ensuing months during which her guest lectures, residencies, and sponsorships dried up almost completely.

As one of those unflinching drug store test wands revealed about seven weeks later, Keff actually got something quite profound out of the conference after all. She didn't expect she'd see Bren again anytime soon, and she honestly didn't particularly care to. Neither their personal or professional lives had brought them into each other's orbit in the previous ten years, and Keff didn't expect that to change. Truthfully, she hoped it wouldn't. Since her early twenties at the latest, Keff had fared quite well with her own resources, and she felt fully prepared to raise her child without a partner if it came to that. She had the support of her family and her local society, and she'd never been faced with having to downgrade her coffee brand or her designer handbag subscription.

Incidentally, Bren claimed not to have noticed the flax motif, nor any of its adulterated successors on the levels above. If nothing else would have, that left her cold in the end.

Still, Keff's leading a classroom-size group through an exclusive corn maze reproduction today, isn't she? Anyone whose credentials checked out would've had to wait at least months for just a couple piddling hours in the corn maze to complete whatever research it was they'd proposed to the academic community. Keff had been bumped up in line for her couple piddling hours. That certainly says something. At least one influential person on some relevant board out there still values her work and her continuing contribution to terrestrial sociology.

Her confidence renewed for the time being, Keff plows on ahead.

"Nyl?" peeps a voice from the back, "If you're still going to the Steam Room tonight, I'll come along."

Keff thinks it's Menderson, the soft-spoken broad-chested man who's altogether too invested in his relationship with his maternal grandparents. This overture, however, is soon swept aside by everyone including Nyl herself, who actually screams a strange incoming-artillery-shell sort of scream at that moment.

As they turn a corner onto what's supposed to be an approach to the exit, they arrive instead at a dead end where a pneumatic scarecrow prop rears up and cackles at them.

Keff all but spears her own thigh with her fork in exasperation. "Sorry . . . I'm sorry. Right, this is the Hampton Corn Palace corn maze, and I was thinking of the Silage of Versailles corn maze for the last several turns there."

Ugh. Rookie mistake. She was distracted, of course, thinking about her career. Keff sighs to herself. With the sorry state her crew's in, they may actually have to be airlifted out of here.

K eff had recognized the syntax of the ad first, rather than any of its semantic content. It was a few weeks ago now that she'd spotted it.

"I'm trying to be your doula," the ad had begun. Based on the limited circulation of the paper and when the ad had appeared, she knew it was written by Feld Deerhold, in spite of how little sense that made.

She'd met Feld in high school, and had previously heard this expression from him in phrases like "I'm trying to be in your lab group for the pig dissection," or "I'm trying to get invited along whenever you guys go to the movies". It was like an admission of effort, and it was endearing in a way. It was rare that anyone she encountered ever wanted to let on that they were expending any sort of special effort for practically anything. In fact, Feld used this "I'm trying" expression in the same context in which other people would use "I'm *not* trying" to do whatever it was.

She'd called the number she had for Feld rather than the one that appeared in the ad. Sure enough, it was he who'd placed it. She asked him to be her doula as long as they could discover exactly what it was a doula did together. Feld's schedule had been wide open, and he accepted his first client there on the spot for the fee she'd offered.

It wasn't that Keff and Feld had been friends, exactly. It was more that he looked up to her and that they'd lived three houses away from each other at that time. When Keff moved to attend college, the nature of their relationship was such that she hadn't thought to tell him goodbye. Almost three years ago now, she'd moved back to her hometown in order to help her parents reach their late-life potential. She could do her main work from almost anywhere, after all, and she'd always liked all the big trees around here too.

Feld and Keff held their initial doula-and-client meeting at her house. On that occasion, they'd briefly interviewed each other:

Feld married a woman from a school district which was the main athletic competition for his own. On their first date, they'd each coincidentally worn jerseys from their respective high school teams, and bonded over recalling cheerleader chants from each side which disparaged the opposing team. Over the next seven years, they'd had two kids and then separated. They divorced six months after the separation. Not long after the divorce, Feld's landscaping business was edged out altogether by an outfit with bigger mowers and better-looking workers, and so he'd reinvented himself. His brother had given him a video game that simulated a birthing ward. One day, when all his other games had been played out, Feld fired up the birthing ward game and played it the entire ensuing week. When he was finished, Feld's was the highest score the creators had ever seen, and they posted a featured blog entry on their site about it. Keff never ascertained if this is what inspired his career switch, but Feld had gone on to community college after that and was now something called a "certified birth doula".

Keff, for her part, had matriculated to Ack Tarminy on a scholarship, and had declared a maritime sociology major straightaway. Only a couple years in, and she was getting her work published in the leading journals. She'd logged a semester in Hawkland Sound doing work on the design and placement of navigational buoys. Another semester was spent determining the psychologically optimal lifeboat deployment for a fleet of passenger oceangoers. Yet another semester found her in Kalevo Bay helping to introduce a non-addictive beverage alternative to grog among jobbing deckhands, which was designed to achieve the same sensations of well-being and communion with the sea.

Some years passed as Keff continued on into a grad program at the school. In the meantime, a groundswell of interest had built surrounding the 200-year-old wreck of the Phrastic Brigantine which came to a head when a well-funded marine exploration company won a contract to salvage it. Ack Tarminy came up in an associated collegiate lottery, and Keff was the shoo-in selection for the mission's marine sociologist. No one was prepared when the Phrastic's hold was breached and crate after crate, the wreck's entire cargo, was prised open to reveal still another pallet of plastic drinking straws. About five-million of them, all told. Unfortunately, it seems, no amount of preparation would have changed anything for Keff. A storm had developed shortly after the final chest had been craned onto the deck, its contents revealed to be drinking straws, same as all the others, and they'd begun the day's journey back to port. Keff was as demoralized by the disappointing recovery as any of the crew were and, to the bosun's chagrin once he'd found out about it, she'd spent the first moments of the storm on deck, lashed to the door of the deckhouse with a thick leather strap in order to accept, as she'd put it, the "castigation of the sea". A mountainous black wave swamped the deck and knocked Keff unconscious for several seconds.

Once she'd come to and wiped the seawater from her eyes, she underwent the first panicked moments of experiencing the sight of anyone's face rendered in blur, as if her eyes were still full of the stinging brine whenever she was face-to-face with someone. As the days passed and the condition sustained, Keff discovered that other materials which would legally identify an individual person were similarly befogged, as if by sea spray. Only her own countenance remained unobscured to herself. In spite of this eccentric affliction which some types of doctors were calling "idiosyncratic prosopagnosia" and other types of doctors were calling a "glitchy enneagram", Keff had buttressed her academic credentials, done a neat pivot, and was now a lettered "terrestrial sociologist".

During that first doula-and-client meeting, Feld had showed Keff what he called the "koala bear", in which they both sat on the floor arranged something like a couple of stacked plastic lawn chairs, Feld as the "back of [Keff's] chair", and they synchronized their breathing. After about five minutes of this, Keff got up and remarked that this wasn't the sort of thing she needed a doula for. She said she'd come to Feld's place for their next meeting. Now, two weeks later, here she was.

Feld has an apartment in an area where most of the buildings are made of green brick. It has something to do either with the sort of clay they quarry around here, or some additives they use in the process. With the aluminum flashing and green brick façade, the building looks like a boarding house for storybook woodland-creature pensioners. This is Keff's first impression, anyway. As Feld buzzes her in and she makes her way along the meatloaf-smelling hallways and stairwells, she's granted an aural insight into the various apartment units. As she moves past the doors on the way to Feld's, she hears conversation in guttural undertones as she passes one door, at least five small children imitating the sound of seabirds as she passes another, the operation of an appliance that's got to be designed either for removing the bones from a turkey, or for inserting a cobra skeleton into a molded gelatin-salad ring for stability as she passes a third, and on it goes as she walks steadily toward Feld's door-number, 593-Z.

A rhyming apartment number, Keff thinks. What a joke.

She finds the door and hears a couple voices excitedly discussing the finish on a bathtub. TV, obviously. She knocks, and a separate voice tells her to come on in.

It's pub-dim in here. The texture of the wall-to-wall carpet is echoed in the stucco ceiling. There's both a banner on the wall over the TV set and a foam finger on a chair in the corner which read "GO CABALLEROS!" Feld is sitting on an overstuffed faux-leather couch eating plain soda crackers and watching some kind of home improvement program on TV. He greets her cheerily and finally gets up to welcome her, but is careful not to give her a hug after their last meeting. Feld's face is blurred to Keff, of course, but she has no doubt it's him. As usual, the blur follows Feld's face around no matter in which direction or at what speed he moves.

"Hi, Doula Deerhold," Keff says with a smirk. "I'm not sure it's a title or not. 'Doula'?"

Immediately, something which sounds just like a sneeze comes from the adjoining kitchenette.

"What was that?" Keff asks. "Is there someone else here?"

"Oh, must be Frank Labodachik, huh? Your parents ever try that one out on you when you were a kid? Frank Labodachik's the guy who's sneezed in a dark room adjoining a lighted room when you go in to investigate the sound of a sneeze and no one's there."

"What?" Keff laughs in spite of herself.

"Yeah, just kidding. No one else's here. I'm pretty sure it's an overactive defrost heater. I've got to call the landlord about it. Hope it won't be too distracting for you."

"No, don't worry about it," Keff says, surveying the garish memorabilia in various places around the small room. "You probably realize I'm less interested in a completely neutral environment than I am in one which reveals the people who put it to daily use. That's partly why I suggested meeting at your place."

"Yeah, I hear that," Feld says quizzically. "Sorry. I'm drinking beer. It's lager. I got you a six-pack too if you'd care to partake. Yours is non-alcoholic."

"Sure," Keff says. "I'll have some. This is important, I think, hanging out like this. I think a doula is mostly supposed to support you emotionally, so this is good. I was reading a little bit about it. A doula's also normally expected to interpret your needs as you're approaching labor or are in labor, and relay that interpretation to the obstetrician."

"Well, yeah," Feld balances the remote control on his wrist. "I mean, I *am* certified and all that. Anyway, I've already done this sort of thing with my wife. I've got an eight- and an eleven-year-old. Don't worry. I know where all the bathrooms and vending machines are at Gerder General."

"Okay. Point taken. Just making conversation." Keff takes a fork from her purse and lays it on the arm of the couch. "She's your *ex*-wife, yeah? A couple weeks ago you'd mentioned you were divorced."

"Well yeah, obviously. No ring. As a certified birth doula, your own marital status is none of my business."

"Alright. I'm fine with that."

They sit and watch the home renovation show for about an hour without any further comment. Keff's mind begins to wander, and she wonders if Nonny got around to picking up the crockery she'd left out on the porch for her. She's just opened her third non-alcoholic beer when she realizes Feld's talking to her. He's talking over the program, somewhat to Keff's annoyance. In some respects, Feld's worse than a husband, and in others he's better. He would never be just as a husband would be, though. At a previous time, Keff had carefully reviewed her attitudes and feelings about Feld, just to be sure, and all she came away with was what she called "beige" which, to her, was the least connotative of colors.

"Sorry, what was that?"

"I said I love how in-depth they get on this show," Feld says, cracking a peanut on a TV tray with the remote control. "This one is always only about renovating bathrooms."

"Wow. Yeah, I was wondering if maybe the hosts got locked in there."

"Nope," Feld replies, choosing to disregard any sarcasm that may have been implied. "The main guy in this show, that guy there, and . . . there. Him. He invented a way to paint cars based on how bathtub mold propagates."

"Okay . . . Tell me more."

"There's this one species of tub mold which spreads its colony out geometrically. Apparently it's like a whisper-chain in grid, whispering itself into existence in all the adjacent directions it doesn't already occur in. Without whispering, of course."

"So he's chosen to paint cars with this method?" Keff looks to be on the verge of saying something completely different. "Paint cars, I mean, rather than using it to repair internal organs in situ, say, or to perform industrial repairs in places that are either dangerous or impossible for people to access?"

"Well, yeah." Feld levers another beer cap off with the edge of the remote control. "I mean, it's not *robotic* mold, or anything. It's actual mold."

"Oh, so you're talking about a person who covers cars in mold."

"It really works, though. Takes about a week altogether, but it gets really even coverage. He treats it afterward, and it sets. It looks good. Only problem is the limited color selection . . . The treatment's available in a spectrum of blacks, browns, greens, and blues."

"Wow," Keff grins, "You had me going there for a minute, doula."

"Stop calling me doula."

"Okay, doula."

"It's not a title."

Another sneeze comes from the depths of the unlit kitchenette.

"Oh boy," Keff yawns, "Hope Frank Labodachik's covering his mouth in there."

L eft turn.
Right turn.
Left turn here at the yellow dumpster.

Alleyways are a lot more colorful, speaking in terms of wavelength, than people normally give them credit for. Weaving in and out of this tucked-away thoroughfare after dark is every bit as vibrant as strolling down the high street at noon. Colors along these back ways, however, have an inverse connotation from the boulevard. Here, blue is silence, green is circumspection, red is a furtive signal from a doorway.

Right turn.
Right turn.
A sprint across a private drive.

Feld's got this byzantine project which he's kept secret from Keff and everybody else. He figures that someday he'll surprise her with the finished product and that she'll actually be impressed. At this rate, though, it may be about a decade before it's done. What it is, is that he's mapping the city's alleyways. Eventually, he'll get to all of them. He's leaving out the public streets so that the map'll sort of depict the city's skeleton. Feld figures this activity is high-falutin enough to merit interest from the right sorts of people. That alone makes it worth it. The only problem is that the goal of the project, the nature of the map, keeps evolving, so he might have to redo a lot of it.

Left turn.
Right turn.

A pause here for bearings-gathering underneath a fire escape that looks like it's made from a jumble of old shopping carts and walking frames.

Feld holds a tactical flashlight between his teeth, draws another right-angle path on the graph paper he's got temporarily propped on a cooling unit, and scribbles some notes. He'd begun this project a few days after his first meeting with Keff. He likes her, sure, and he wants her to like him too. More than that though, he wants her to recognize something he's done completely on his own as a thing of merit. In fact, he wants that in general. Really what it is, Feld supposes, is that he wants to cultivate a community of peers. That's not all there is to it, of course. Otherwise, why would he have spent these two-to-three hours after dark three times a week these last several weeks? Why would he feel so assured that he'll continue with the project for as long as it takes to complete it properly? No, this is actually something that *should* be accomplished. People like those he's trying to count himself one of just have these sorts of convictions about things.

A simple map doesn't possess enough relevance, though, even if it *is* a new map. Now that the whole world's mapped, new maps are only a matter of granularity. Feld's conundrum here is illustrated by considering the difference between a draftsman and an architect. Basically, it's that no one will ever smash down the iron door to the chamber of influence with a T-square and some French curves. Feld had realized this stuff about relevance and influence within the first couple weeks he'd spent on the project. His initial thought was to add zoning to his maps which expanded the existing "residential", "commercial", "industrial" zoning of the city. He'd had an intuition that the zoning of a system of streets running between and oblique to the public streets, that is to say *alleyways,* would be completely independent from the familiar notions of the way structures are used. After a few nights of coding his map with zones, however, it seemed more like an administrative task than anything. Coming across as an administrator would have been worse than simply acting the part of the draftsman.

Feld's idea now is to code sections of alleyway as "functional", "dysfunctional", or "hybrid". He's got a nebulous idea about how this system would look in terms of city planning, but he'd prefer to think of it in *societal* terms. That's really what ought to impel city planning anyway, oughtn't it? The degree of productive use to which a society puts a municipal system?

Finishing up his notes for now, Feld stows the tactical light, steps over a mosaic of broken liquor-bottle glass, and heads on to the next block. These are the faces of buildings that most people don't see, and this truth is either plainly acknowledged or politely disregarded in the design of the rear façade. On this block, for example, the building backs look like the sides of ocean liners. They're smooth-faced, with mysterious geometric recesses here and there employed, doubtlessly, in the care and feeding of these inscrutable whitewashed monoliths. A smear of interior light spreads across a section of slick pavement, and Feld edges up to the window to have a look.

Inside is a cavernous glass-walled boardroom. There are about ten people, top executive types from the look of them, working late. They're assembled around a table topped with marbled glass in brown, gray, and black, intently watching projections of animated explosive logos of the company's name on a high-res wall-filling screen. In any case, the name displayed in the acrobatic logos is the same name spelled out in reflective letter stickers on the deliveries door a couple meters from the window's edge where Feld secretly observes. As the rainbow colors pulse and the starbursts glow on the screen, Feld holds completely still waiting to see what will happen next. As several minutes pass, the execs remain fixed on the display, and the logos continue to scintillate. There are no pauses to confer. There is no rhythm of narration in the presentation that Feld can discern, yet the windows buzz slightly with the frequencies of rumbling sound effects which line up with particularly showy pyrotechnics that the motion graphics undertake.

With a sudden flash of inspiration, Feld fumbles in a back pocket and withdraws the remote control he's taken to superstitiously carrying along with him. From beyond the window, he points it at the presentation in the boardroom, and he presses the power button.

The screen goes immediately dark and silent. A moment passes in which Feld isn't sure whether he's stifling a yelp of panic or a roar of mirth. Still the execs remain seated and unspeaking, none of them making a move to fix the display or to account in any way for the failure of their screen. A woman in a gray jacket and skirt jogs her papers together on the table and sets them back down.

Unbelievingly, Feld walks into view of the window and waves exaggeratedly, waggling the remote control above his head. The shadow of a scowl passes across the face of a man oriented across the room from him, but then the fellow goes back to gazing at nothing in particular.

Grunting to himself, Feld presses on. Holding his graph paper stiffly in one hand, he marks a sloppy "D" for "dysfunctional" on this part of his map.

Another few meandering blocks, a few angular marks on his graph paper, and Feld draws up short at a soot-encrusted window. Something about the way the combination of colors and shapes inside stimulates the edge of his eye makes him stop to look. It appears to be a bar or some sleazy private social club. About twenty-odd mill around an amber-lit room in nothing but white towels. The interior looks to have been a deli at one time, and has been only incompletely converted into whatever sort of place this is. The counter is being used as a bar, the wall's still full of nails which once must have supported framed photos of those clientele who were able to eat the deli's legendary giant sandwich in one sitting, and the room is lined with cast-iron radiators. Feld marks a spidery "H" on his map for "hybrid", and a moment later adds a question mark after it.

On a whim, Feld points his remote control into the room at nothing in particular, and presses a button. The music changes to something more lively, and a cluster of people who'd been casually talking begin to dance. After a few minutes of this, Feld, feeling mischievous, incrementally increases the volume. The dancers' movements become more energetic and insistent. A woman who reminds Feld of his fourth grade teacher, complete with terrier hair, stumpy limbs, and large teeth begins spinning around with her arms up in the air while the other dancers pause to watch and to cheer her on. Without warning, a metallic knocking sound commences which is out of time with the music. While some look around to discover the source of the noise, a sudden small burst of movement catches Feld's attention, and the woman's white towel cascades to the floor. At the very moment, a terrific jet of water vapor erupts from a valve in one of the radiators, and the woman looses a scream like a steam whistle. Startled, Feld accidentally hits another button on the remote, and the music is replaced with the grating voice of a talk-radio blowhard. Shaken, Feld hurries on.

As Feld continues along this unending network of obscure walkways, the moon shifts in the sky. He gets lost, recognizes a cluster of dumpsters, and then gets lost again. When once more he knows where he is, he's standing in the alleyway that runs along the back of Keff Stewart's house. He didn't mean to end up here. Not really. He and Keff had never set up their next meeting, and he hasn't heard from her in about a month. The last time they spoke was when she'd stopped by his apartment that once. Her due date's just a few weeks away, but every time he calls her, it seems the call gets sent to voicemail after one or two rings. He's really got to make a better and more consistent effort at this doula thing, he thinks. Out of concern, and somewhat out of curiosity, he peers in the window.

Keff's watching TV in the dark. It looks to be a movie with lots of trees and streetlights. Feld, viewing from the window, gets caught up in the movie. The trees and streetlights begin whizzing by, and then they're replaced by moonlight through the slats of a fence, and then marshy reeds and flitting moths. It's almost like he and Keff are watching the movie together. It's like they've *arranged* to watch it together in the same room is what Feld means.

Feld suddenly feels very tired. He aims his remote and presses, and Keff stretches and yawns. He flinches when she calls to someone in the other room. Her voice modulates differently than he'd remembered. He presses again, and a sneeze sounds from a far room. Feeling skeptical, he aims the remote once more and gives it an emphatic jab. The light in the room comes on. Keff's flipped the switch. Now she's standing up, alert and unbending, and is looking intently toward the window Feld's hiding just outside of.

Feld holds his breath and turns invisible. The moon shifts again.

The sedan with the different-colored doors makes its way tentatively across the rutted sward. It passes a stand of trees and the branches twist crazily in glass and chrome reflection, as if the sedan isn't versed in rendering these objects of the open land. The vehicle stops several yards beyond a barbed-wire-topped chain-link fence as tall as a bus which stretches in both directions as far as can be seen. There's a vast cornfield on the opposite side of the fence.

The car stereo continues to play. It's a feature story delivered in a broadcast-journalism voice:

After decades of unsuccessful attempts, the wreck divers ultimately breached the ancient wooden ship. A confluence of technology and bull-headedness finally produced this first successful mission.

The Phrastic Brigantine was wrought of stout wood, fasted heartily to its framework with handmade nails and a thick slathering of pine tar. Having spent the better part of a bi-century in a deep-fathom harbor, this engineering marvel was now garlanded with florets and arabesques of barnacles and limpets which covered the length of even its tallest mast.

The sunken ship's cargo was stored in a dozen watertight chests, each about the size of a sarcophagus, but cuboid in shape, and constructed sturdily on the same building principle as the ship itself.

When the first chest was craned onto the deck of the huge research vessel, every bit steel and high-function polymer as the ship beneath was wood and iron, it was opened with the utmost care.

Inside was cardboard crate upon cardboard crate of translucent-plastic drinking straws.

Over the next few days, the remaining chests were carefully recovered and opened, and their cargo was just the same as the first.

All in all, the stout wooden wreck contained millions of plastic drinking straws, all of them the same size, shape, and material as the others.

In the succeeding weeks, the rescued drinking straws were shipped off to high school cafeterias all across Maldesia, and through those straws passed untold gallons of chocolate milk, orange juice, and flavored water.

"Dad," a small plaintive voice entreats, "This is the twelfth time we've listened to this one. If we're here, let's just get out."

"Sorry, sorry. You're right. It's related in a way to our outing, though. Wake your brother up, and we'll get going."

Feld exits the sedan and beelines for a gate in the fence that's padlocked shut with heavy chains. There's a boxy security camera mounted atop a stout pole nearby. Feld points his remote control at it and presses, but the red light on the camera remains. In exasperation, he flings the remote end over end at the camera. It hits dead on with a dull clack and whether it's switched something off or broken it, the red light no longer shines.

Within three minutes of the camera going dark, Feld has gotten himself and his kids, Rena and Bant, past the secured gate. Though the area's somewhat overgrown, he's discovered an opening in the corn not far from the entryway.

"You guys like mazes, do ya?"

"Mazes?" Bant, the eleven-year-old, is still groggy having slept most of the two-hour drive. "Like on the backs of cereal boxes and stuff? I mean, I *guess*."

Little Rena smiles and skips along a path in the corn. Soon they arrive at a junction, and the trio stop for a moment.

"So, yeah," Feld begins. "This is a maze one of my clients built. It's an experimental design. The only one of its kind. I think you both know how important this new career is to me, don't you guys?"

"Ummm," Rena chirps, "Mom says you want to hug pregnant ladies?"

"Well, there's a little more to it than that." Feld hikes up his pants and looks nervously back toward the way they'd come. "Anyway, it's important that I get to know my clients, and this is the perfect way for me to get to know this one I'm working with now. Through her work, you know? I mean, going through this maze ought to be fun on top of it all. That's why I brought you guys along. So we can all have fun together. Just like old times, huh?"

"Okay, Dad, I'm on board," Bant pipes. Feld can never tell these days whether the boy's being sarcastic or not. "This first split's got to be left. Haven't you noticed that the first turn along a maze always ends up being a left?"

<<<

Keff scrolls down the web page.

The corn labyrinth is not a corn maze. Here, husks rustle meditatively on cryptic breezes. From a field away, we hearken to train-of-thought tractors ploughing ruminant swaths through the pathscape.

"No, no, no, no. This is garbage. Why the hell would you make a *labyrinth* out of a cornfield?" Keff pounds the end of her take-along fork on the table for emphasis. It was more than a few months ago now that she'd been eating a quick lunch before running out on an errand, and had absentmindedly taken the fork along. It proved so useful on that occasion, that she now just normally had it along, often in her bag. Sometimes though, like now, she had it in-hand. She'd stop carrying it once it became weird.

"Just saying, Keff," the woman sitting across from her opines. "Taking this residency could be your ticket back into the industry."

"Yeah, a ticket for the nosebleeds at a kazoo concert. No thanks."

"Well, it's yours if you'll take it. Ray and I think you should."

"I dunno. I can't think straight right now. Everyone's dumping their shit on me. My former colleagues, the terrestrial sociology department at Tarminy, the custodians of this residency at a so-called corn labyrinth. I'm spammed by humanity, for fuck's sake. You of all people, Nonny? You're supposed to be my moral support through this experience."

"*I'm* supposed to be your support? Do you mean for the revival of your career? For your pregnancy and what comes afterward? I

126

mean, I'm happy to help as much as I can. Anyway, I thought you had a doula."

"Well, I owe him a call." Keff pushes her hair aside, and props the fork behind her ear to keep it in place.

"Okay. In the meantime, Ray and I are more than happy to stop by and help out with whatever."

Keff had agreed to meet Nonny at this coffee shop. It's not the one she normally goes to, and she had to drive past almost an entire village of those green-brick buildings to get here. Ugh. Not the nicest area. Anyway, the coffee's not bad, and Nonny is as stable an influence as ever. Keff needs that right now.

"So," Nonny propounds, "Does your specialist have a plan in place for the . . . face thing?"

"The prosopagnosia?"

"Is that what they've decided it is?"

"Well, yeah. A form of it, anyway. I mean, your face is still blurred to me right now. The lady on the cup's face is." Keff indicates the line-drawn logo on the disposable coffee cup. Social security numbers. License plates. Swimming pool pass IDs."

"Oh, God. Sorry, Keff. I didn't know the half of it."

"Yeah, this specialist I'm seeing now thinks my delivery may actually resolve it. A shock to the system like that, you know? That I'll be able to see my kid's face when it comes out? I'm not sure he's telling me that because he thinks it's what I want to hear . . . Oh . . ."

"Keff? You okay?"

Keff's eyes and mouth are suddenly stuck, fixed, and she's doubled over in her chair. One hand grips the table edge, and the other presses on her stomach-bulge. She sucks in a breath. About three minutes pass while Nonny hovers at her side.

"Okay," Keff says, "I'm pretty sure that was a contraction. I had one last night. I'm fine."

As they pull on their coats and get ready to leave, Keff abruptly crouches down in another paroxysm, her hands bracing against the floor.

Once she stabilizes, Nonny helps her along.

"Alright, we ought to get you to the hospital."

"Okay. Here. Call my doula. Not sure when one of these waves is going to hit again. He's in my address book under 'D'".

> > >

"Dad? Are we almost at the end?" Little Rena stops to pull at a corn husk. They've been in the maze now for about an hour.

"What's that Rena? Ummm, I think so." Feld, for his part, is trying not to broadcast to his kids how frantic he is. They probably think he's a bit of a loser anyway, and it won't help the situation in any case. The time it will take to make the trip back to town wouldn't normally be a deal-breaker on a childbirth timetable, but Keff's designed this maze a little too well. Feld's lost.

"Getting to know your client any better, Dad?" Bant inquires. Okay, Feld thinks. That was definitely sarcasm. It's probably always sarcasm. Remember that, and at least you can save a little face.

For the past twenty minutes Feld's been messaging with some-one on Keff's phone called Nonny who's asked him to meet them at Gerder General right away. Of course, he can't truthfully message back just why that can't happen, but he still half thinks he can get there in time too, so he's deflecting and stalling. The messages on Nonny's end have been getting increasingly aggressive and dismissive at the same time.

When he looks back up from his phone, it's only Rena standing there in front of the rustling stalks. No Bant.

"Rena, honey, where's Bant?"

"Oh, I thought you heard him, Dad. He said he was going on ahead to find the way out and then he's going to come back and get us. He's only been gone a few minutes."

Feld passes a hand over his face and melts into the ground. The stalks rustle again.

< < <

As her epidural kicks in, Keff thinks about how to a lot of peo-ple, even to some designers themselves, it doesn't matter that it's corn that makes up the maze. To them, corn's a building material like any other with its own advantages and drawbacks . . . It *does* matter that it's corn, though. You're not going to design the same twists and turns through corn that you would through straw bales or through a brick passageway. A lot of people don't seem to understand that.

How odd. Like thinking about the deployment of consumer electricity while competing in a prizefight, or about political motivations while riding a plummeting roller coaster. Sometimes grounding or centering thoughts really are strictly conceptual in nature.

Keff gazes at a face-blob connected to an arm, and from there to a hand that's holding hers. She's pretty sure it's Nonny. That's good. She likes Nonny.

Another pause, and a great wave of generative decree passes through Keff's frame. She gives a twisting heave on the natal bed, and in that interval goes from taut and stifled to clear and serene. A squalling peal fills the room, and a small writhing shape is placed on Keff's chest which she views through a sheen of tears.

A newsstand puzzle book rustles on a table across the room in the air current of a briskly-passing obstetrician who exchanges a smile with the delivery nurse. Wagers exchange hands at the sidelines of nature and society, and the world turns.

PERIOD PIECE

{DISCOVERY:}

The first thing that strikes one is the absence of practically any industry-wrought color in the red-orange-yellow half of the visible light rainbow. There are some washed-out greens verging on pallid yellow, but most of the things people make are only the color of the hair, hide, wood, stone, or iron they're made from.

The next thing one notices is how feeble the radiations and other signals are that industry is able to muster. Send up a marsh-gas-filled balloon stitched from the desiccated stomachs of all the large game that was brought down in the season's hunt. Get it up as high as the clouds and look down. One observes very little light. Contrive an ear trumpet as large as a siege engine, and stretch a fresh elastic rat's hide at its listening end. One observes very little vibration.

No surprise, really. This is a period piece, after all.

So then, the bed Torry Ninekin reclines on is only the color of the linen from which the mattress and pillowcases are spun, only the color of the cypress from which the bed frame is hewn. Her bedmate is only the colors of the skin and hair with which he was born. The only sounds are the small rodents skittering here and there, some washwater dripping in a nearby room, and a rhythmic hammering from somewhere farther away. The funfair won't open this morning for another several hours yet.

It's still nearly lightless in the chamber this early in the morning. Torry's lately taken to hanging a tigerskin across the door opening, and balancing a couple staves against it which will clatter to the floor and scare off any inquisitive chamberlains or preceptors who may happen along. Earlier in the season, depending on how affected she was by whomever it might have been, she may have invited them in, but that often provoked more trouble than it was worth. The night the funfair opened, the spring equinox, Torry had returned to her chamber at dawn with a milkmaid and a stableman. In his avidity, the stableman dealt the girl a blow so vicious that it changed the profile of her face. As the poor lass sat screaming and holding bloodied bedclothes to herself, Torry grasped the stableman securely by the hair, sliced his ear off in a single clean stroke, and physically ejected him from the room, throwing the ear after. She thought she'd seen him once since, but the fellow made no attempt to renew their acquaintanceship.

These last several days, Torry's curtailed her adventures as per her customary practice this close to an installation. Postas Dendo, the current bedmate, had attached himself to her a few days ago, and that was fine. Postas clearly had no idea what he wanted any further than a week away from each new day. He was comely, with large eyes, full lips, and slender limbs. Whenever it would facilitate, he knew how to explain his feelings about things. Best of all, he wasn't dogmatic. In any case, Torry would be completing her work for the Shahdom here within the day, and would then continue southward along the amber road toward the next HomeHub.

Torry lies half-awake now, face-to-face with Postas, playing a game they'd recently devised whose uncomplicated object is trying to determine if the other's eyes are open or closed in the near-light-lessness. Over the last days, they'd discovered that they rose in the morning at roughly the same time. They'd taken to lying there with eyes open once they woke, not saying anything, not altering their position, staring as long as they were able before the strangeness of it overcame one of them and the game was ended. Before the sun's fully above the trees, it's actually a challenge discerning whether a pair of eyes even a hairsbreadth from your own are closed or staring. Torry judges, abetted by Postas' slow measured breathing, that his eyes are closed for now. She closes her own eyes again and thinks back to her dream, activating her own perspective in the process.

I launch a recollection of last night's dream. I'm back at my birth home, barely old enough to flesh a chinkara, two or three days into one of my ritual walkabouts. The forest here is self-similar and inscrutable. An ability to get unlost is the only thing that would ever permit an exit from such a place. In accord with my birthright, I *have* cultivated an ability to get unlost. To do so now, I limit my viewfield to nine trees at any one time and always keep to the right of those five trees in that viewfield whose lotería combination is least auspicious. I weave to the left of a "fish" tree, then, and to the right of a "requital" and a "fathoms" tree grown together at the bole. Some minutes later, I bear *right* of a "fish" tree, recontextualized as it is in the presence of a "jammed pistol" and "spleen" tree.

Another hour of this sigil-steering, and the trees start to thin. I emerge from the forest into a landscape completely novel to me in its lushness. A panorama of gently rolling hills spreads before me. Everything is covered in short springy grass; a green so vivid I'd only ever previously seen its like in a carefully assayed dye-pulp of weld and indigo.

In a grassy hollow, about as far away from me as one end of a banqueting hall is from its opposite end, I see a small splash of contrasting color which interrupts the green monotony all around, and so I head for it. As I approach this inconsistency, I realize it's a shock of colorful bloom whose flowers are so deeply red that they appear almost black.

Scarcely thinking what I'm doing, I uproot the bloom, and am immediately encompassed and confined within a pillar of red-black; neither the forest nor the grass anywhere to be discerned. What's more, I appear to possess only a *perspective* here. The rest of me, the husk, has been shucked somewhere between the bloom-plucking and now. I can observe, but I have no opinion about or emotional engagement with my situation. I have only the most rudimentary sense of intent.

From the series of sonar probes I've been permitted to emit by sheer will alone, I've determined that the pillar has a square cross-section with an interior wall-to-opposite-wall dimension about the length of a snooker cue, and that it appears to be constructed from large stone blocks. If it has a floor or ceiling, they're beyond the reach of my probes. There's a stout iron chain which seems it should run the expanse of the entire pillar. The chain's pulled fairly taut, and sometimes it will quiver as if thrummed or otherwise manipulated somewhere along its length; this manipulation having originated, perhaps, at a considerably earlier (historic) time from somewhere far away up or down the pillar.

I may as well let you know that I've lost track of how long I've helmed this perspective inside the pillar. It may have been several consecutive childhoods at this point.

There's also an unglazed window in the wall of the shaft, beyond which usually shines a pallid blue-white light. The light may either be actual daylight, or some *construct* of daylight such as the sort of light which emits from a celestial carriage. I sometimes hear sounds from this window. They're always outdoor sounds, something like the sound of a village square and adjoining green engaged in bloody revolution. I hear death cries, shouts of victory and solidarity, companies of troops singing various sectarian anthems as they march, along with all the attendant multi-story wood-bronze-iron machinery of these sounds. Other times I hear nothing, no matter how hard I strain my relevant sense-constructs. If the unglazed window *does* let out onto an outdoor vista anything like the intermittent sounds suggest, I'd likely hear insects and birds, carts being drawn down cobbled streets, wind-flapped pennants, and the like. At these other times, however, I hear nothing at all.

Over the last several minutes, years, or childhoods, whichever it may be, I've discovered I can change my orientation by imagining a loom's spinning wheel and by rotating it. The wheel itself lacks the creature presence of a real-life object. In my visualization, the spinning wheel is gray and moss-textured, a shade within shadows, but it suffices. Every time it makes a revolution, I travel the length of a banqueting hall along the pillar, and my visual perspective makes a complete turn perpendicular to the pillar's length. In this manner, I am always faced directly away from the unglazed window whenever I'm level with it. I seem to have no control over this. What's more, I've tried turning the wheel interminably in one direction, and I've never encountered a second opening. I'd nearly lost track of the one window with that maneuver. Turned clockwise, I travel in one direction along the inside of the pillar, and anticlockwise I travel the opposite.

At some advanced time, I make an important discovery. On one side of the window, aurally, it seems I'm in the midst of the revolutionaries, and on the other side, also aurally, I'm in the midst of the constabulary and the loyalists. Sometimes, I'll turn the spinning wheel one way past the window and then the other, back and forth, trying to discern an interchange between the two assemblages, but there's never an evident call and response as far as I can tell. Perhaps the two assemblages don't articulate at the same occasion or accommodation.

At a time even further advanced than this, I comprehend that "perspective" is never wholly disembodied. I understand, then, that I still possess a hand which grasps the red-black bloom from the hollow. In my frustration at how long this comprehension has taken to develop, I crush the bloom. Once again, I am in the glade. The forest looms at my back. I disengage from the dream memory and from my own perspective.

Torry lies musing, eyes closed, on a cypress-framed bed in a complex of the fledgling HomeHub of Terra Termina, the very end of the line in terms of geography, culture, and concept.

"Hey," a grizzled yet ephebic voice accosts. "You're playing the game wrong. If you're awake, your eyes should be opened."

"New rules," Torry whispers, and vaults across Postas in a single movement to the smooth stone floor. In almost the same moment, the staves balanced on the tigerskin door-cover clatter to the floor, and a pair or two of footsteps scuttle off down the hall.

"You'd think a body'd never had any fun in bed," Torry remarks. "Alright, then. I've got to go supervise the installations, make a few remarks, do some consecrations, the whole bit, and then I'm off, back from the end of the world." She pulls on a tunic that says "LIVING IMAGE" across the front, wriggles into some breeches, and begins the arduous process of binding the modular leather thongs to her feet which go for shoes in this period. "You've been great these last few days, Postas," she says. "You really have. Better than most. I'd like to see you one last time, so I'll stop down to the funfair on my way along to say a proper goodbye."

Before Postas can adequately wipe the sleep from his eyes or make any sort of gesture one way or the other, Torry's echoing down the hall, having taken the staves, the tigerskin, and a few other personal items along with her.

Torry's wintered here in Terra Termina, but now with the solstice funfair having begun, the weather having decidedly broken, she's duty bound as an appointed officer of the realm. She's meant to continue her circuit, HomeHub to HomeHub, acting as the roving ideologist, tastemaker, and occult sensitive of the Shah.

In short, she's one of a very select feudal class of poster vendors. Along with vintners and preceptors, the poster vendor is highly learned and articulate, and is expected to deal directly with the highest-ranking officials and nobles of the land. The poster vendor is also charged with acting as a curator of culture and personal anecdote as it relates to travels between the most lateral and medial nodes of the Shahdom.

Torry quits the dormitory and crosses a courtyard whose nod to the decorative is prescriptive and austere. There's an edged border along which concrete garlands, all cast of the same mold, are mounted at regular intervals. A few small wooden buildings here have zigzag cornices of the like seen in several HomeHubs across the Shahdom, signifying the alternating universal epochs of development and inertia. Most surfaces are painted, but the paint this period and locale has conjured or preserved thus far comes only in the scungiest tones of brown, green, and gray. She walks past a broomsquire she's seen there a few times lashing his broomcorn to whittled branches and standing the finished brooms together on end. He smiles cautiously at her, flickeringly, and tries not to gawk.

Finally, she reaches her ambulant portmanteau stored safely away in a shingled outbuilding. The portmanteau is something like a caravan without a cabin, or a large wardrobe turned on its back with wagon wheels added. It's got a bulbous assembly at one end with a flue on top and, just forward of that, an unadorned coxswain's pew with a helm connected to a steering linkage. Some of the Shah's finest engineers helped Torry wrangle the thing from its elements. Whenever she's in the presence of the portmanteau, it precipitates a tickle of autonomy in herself, as well as a flutter of accountability. This time, it also causes her to smile thoughtfully.

She unlocks a panel which runs the length of the portmanteau, draws it back, and begins riffling through one stack of the hundreds of posters therein. At this point, making the appropriate selections won't take long. Torry's sung the songs of this place, drunk its potions, and picked its scabs going on now the better part of a season. Many evenings she's spent with the mater and pater of the HomeHub holding forth on matters of town, country, and dosshouse, taking part with them in all manner of dubious contests and vulgar amusements in counterpoint to the squalls and ructions rattling the greathall's fittings for days at a time. The mater and pater are a young couple with one infant, and another on the way. The mater is the Shah's niece, so their footing is well-fixed, especially in a place as far-removed from everything else as this one is. There's every reason to believe they'll enjoy long abundant lives.

Torry's been working her final selections to the top of the pile for the past weeks. She carefully draws out a poster, holds it at arm's-length, and sizes it up. It's a popular one across the Shahdom. It depicts a fortress dwarfing the mountains and the sun. The legend "KEEP THE PEACE" is printed below. She sets this one carefully atop the portmanteau and draws the next. This one illustrates a famous scene from a play that has surely been performed, probably several times, as part of any HomeHub's entertainments. It pictures a patrician woman stripped of her finery standing in a woodland, one raised hand full of glowing stars, and one lowered hand grasping a voluminous book. Printed below is "THE CHOICE: HOMEHUB OSCURO, FALL EQUINOX '38". Torry flips to her final selection, and then flips past it. On an informed whim, she withdraws a print she'd passed over several times until now. It pictures a tall tree throwing a long shadow whose tip is right at the edge of a lone pavilion in the wilderness. She places the poster on the portmanteau's broad surface, fits a large nib to a dowel and dips the assembly into a jar of gall and gum she has on hand. With a few deft strokes, she sketches a brazier as tall as a flagpole between the tree and the pavilion, within which she places a blazing globe of flame. Finished now, she fans her work dry, stacks the posters, rolls them loosely together, and cradles the tube under her arm.

Turning about, she carefully takes the main HomeHub building in one last time, shielding her eyes from the murky sunlight. Here at Terra Termina, the sun is perpetually either in rise or set mode. It never fully dips below the horizon or rises very far above the distant trees. This landmark Torry gazes upon represents the most grasping reach of the Shah's, or anyone's, influence. Some dozen childhoods ago, the HomeHub here was established as part of a realm-sponsored expedition. The library, still the most imposing building in the complex, was constructed from the stout timber of the forest trees. Nearly every exterior surface was faced with graphite from a local quarry all that time ago, and the facing's nearly all still in place. The current tenants have made the joke about its being essentially a giant pencil, but the edifice really does have an aspect of majesty to it. The original library collection remains, more or less. Most of the books are about quarrying and drilling, but there are also several novels whose popularity and relevance peaked about four childhoods past.

The library, then, is a carven pedestal set on a substantial base which is something like a geometrically rectified version of one of those brittle-skeletoned sea brooches with radiating arms. The structure's black and glossy, and nearly as big as a galleon. The rosy effluvia of oblique sunlight radiates on the haunches of an ambush of molded tigers, which are crafted of the same glossy black as the library. There are twelve tigers fanned out around the building, flanking each of the twelve entrances, each doing half-duty guarding two entrances. Twelve, the number of kingdoms in the Shahdom and flashes across the Shah's command jacket, is assumed to confer a numerological benefit here at this remote enterprise. Since its completion, the building's been subtly modified by oldtime forces, stressed and flexed by the peculiar tectonics of this promontory of all civilization. It would seem the designers had a measure of architectural savvy. They've allowed for the building to remake itself this way and to look all the more foreboding-majestic-inviting, as ambivalent as are its books, media, and its very reason for being taken as a whole. The building morphs plausibly with the changes in politics, custom, and taste.

Anyhow, because this place is the way it is, incidentally *not* a library from which you can renew your overdue materials via semaphore relay as you can at most of the others, it possesses a few Numinous Attributes.

One Numinous Attribute is its Readiness. There is a cafeteria in the library which is known for serving small dumplings, manti, whose dough is done up in a particular folding gesture of benediction. The chef obligingly and credulously fills them with anything one may suggest that is to be had to-hand. The chef is a freethinker, not a simpleton, and will make you lay down your coin-of-the-realm in advance if you request a manti stuffed with gunpowder and cockleshells. "Readiness" may help explain why when supply shipments *do* arrive twice or thrice every peaceable season via the tiger-flanked loading dock, they've been known to include items as diverse as fossil fish teeth, porcelain thimbles, and decorative knots tied in worsted yarn.

Another Numinous Attribute is its Inventiveness. Approaching the main entrance, having walked up the glossy-black steps past the inscrutable tigers, one is faced with a potash-paned display case changed equinoctially by the staff. The current display features a mannequin-head likeness of a personality with a huge bouffant and mother-of-pearl-rimmed hazeglasses, with related books and media stood up around it. Green crêpe-paper sea waves beset the display, and stylized verdigris-colored crystal flakes depend from the top of the enclosure. Presumably, these decorations are all relevant to some unifying node, but one wouldn't necessarily know *which* node without most of the disparate decorations in place, and may not know anyway. Honestly, my guess is it's one of those bigger-than-being wharf cocks of that bright-lights city known today as Lampersveldt.

One more Numinous Attribute for now is the library's Conclusiveness. This is the last frontier for a lot of things. The HomeHub library at Terra Termina is a place where, if one is ever to connect with a certain person, vision, or concept, one can be confident that this is the only opportunity to do so. There's even a custom here for making such a connection which Torry herself has enacted. On that occasion, she'd promenaded past the sculptural sentinels at the entryway (the lifesize toy soldier, ice robot, scratched-celluloid-stop-motion effigies stood there), on through the heavy felt curtain, and she'd gotten herself in among the stacks. There, in the thick of them, she'd run a finger just so along the leather, pelt, and time-withered-sellotape spines. She'd closed her eyes, twirled around, and then decidedly withdrew a particularly ample volume from the shelf she'd found herself standing in front of. This was how she'd first encountered Postas Dendo, eye-to-eye from one aisle to the next, through the aperture the removed book had left. Of course, Postas knew about the custom too. He could have been spying and have situated himself there just so, but that's not to say that the custom didn't function as it was generally intended to.

With the rolled poster tube under her arm, then, Torry takes her supply sack from the ambulant portmanteau and makes for the library and living quarters of the esteemed family, there for to perform her installations and attendant ceremony, and to enjoy the comforts of this outpost of the Shahdom a final time before continuing along the amber road.

When she exits the library some hours later, having done with her official duties, the sun is at its highest, just brushing the tops of the outlying trees. Torry has suited up for her trip in the garderobe of the building. Now, picking her way back across the courtyard, she causes the broomsquire to blanch. She cuts quite a heathen-looking figure. For one thing, her face is now painted with crushed safflower, ground stibnite, and clotted ochre. She's rendered yellow sunbursts around her eyes, a red chevron across the bridge of her nose, and the whole of her jaw is painted black. She wears a mantle that reaches nearly to her knees which is crafted in patchwork from a variety of hides and pelts in all manner of colors, shapes, and textures. Each of her legs is wrapped in a long strip of scarlet brocade, and an ankle bangle rattles gratingly as she goes.

Torry stows her effects in the portmanteau for the time being, withdraws a bulky valise, and continues past the courtyard on toward the funfair which is set up some 200 paces away. Postas operates the carousel there which is just as well, as she's decided to officially identify the carousel as a protected item in the Dispersed Treasurehouse collection, curated on behalf of the Shah by officials such as herself. What the curation entails is the installation of an indexed geodetic stake at the site, and the creation of an accredited description and image of the item whose record will eventually be presented to the Shah, and finally stored back at his citadel.

As she walks, Torry recalls some of Postas' endearing prattle concerning his funfair chores. Apparently, while the foreman was initially showing Postas the tasks he'd need to perform on his rounds, he'd explained how to check for problems with the guy-wires that stabilize the big attraction tents, he'd showed Postas how to run a couple of the popular rides, and he'd illustrated some principles of crowd control.

When he'd gotten around to the carousel and to explaining some of the things that could go wrong with it, the foreman had acted sheepish and apologetic. He'd explained how the carousel was probably the least popular attraction of the funfair, but that they hadn't yet phased it out altogether for one indistinct reason or another.

The shabby band organ, the carousel's centerpiece, plays reed-organ and rickety percussion versions of tunes that no one has known the words to now for a dozen childhoods and more. What it comes down to, Torry considers, is that she'd been struck by Postas' conviction that sometimes the cultural connection a certain object endows may, at its root, be completely arbitrary. Culture, Postas had declaimed, is a charming vagrant.

The funfair, then, lays before Torry on a slight acclivity. As she approaches, she first glimpses the stunted Ferris wheel with its decrepit baskets nodding like sleepy pensioners. Next, a spire of the candyfloss stand heaves into view whose sugary vendibles are undeviatingly grapefruit sized and shaped, and come in only one shade of pigeon-gray. As she comes level with the funfair plot, Torry takes in all the stimuli we might today associate with a charity carnival situated temporarily in the parking lot of a shopping mall. Those stimuli are replete with a mass of hawkers roaring into treebark megaphones (sounding like nothing so much as insects with lungs the size of wineskins), about an even split between people who appear to be somewhat miffed and those who actually seem to be enjoying themselves, and a faint yet pervasive smell of vomit.

Just like the rest of Terra Termina, this funfair is a place for last chances and reserve-tank providences. Other people's, as well as one's own.

The funfair's installed on an expansive concrete pad which's been poured by the builders of the library. The library constructors had partially erected another building here whose remnants persist. Just beyond the farthest funfair attraction, those remnants comprise a scattering of rusting iron scaffolds and standing pillars faced with sheets of chipped and dented graphite. The pavement here is quite a bit more cracked than similarly-aged pavement, affected no doubt in that peculiar manner by Terra Termina's own wind belts and sun wavelengths. Small succulent tendrils of some purplish herbage push through wherever they might.

Torry ambles over to the carousel where Postas is fiddling with the automatic band organ. Without a word to him, she sets her valise on the ground and withdraws a geodetic stake and a large mallet. After a few minutes of hammering the stake in and anchoring it just so with some iron spikes, she stands back and surveys her work. Satisfied, she removes a black wooden box from the valise, secures it atop a stabilizing rod, lines it up, and presses a shutter button on the side. In a moment, a flat sheet of tin no bigger than the palm of a hand extrudes from a slot at the bottom of the box. Postas watches, captivated, as a distinct image of the carousel with its brand new identifying marker takes shape on the surface of the tin.

"This appliance is on loan from the Shah," Torry quips. She stows the wooden box carefully back in her valise, and closes it up.

Scarcely before she has time to rise to a fully upright position, Torry is accosted by a small rugged-looking man who has a generally weather-crazed look about him. His lips are more livid than they ought to be, and his clothing and hair are full of brambles.

"From Speaker Truzi of HomeHub Emzadi. Lampersveldt town. I'm relieved that I've reached you before you'd gone."

A messenger. He thrusts a sealed bronze capsule into Torry's hand. She breaks the seal, empties four waxen disks into her palm, and joggles them there until she can see all their faces at once. Lotería disks: snake, oast house, fathoms, and induction.

"I won't be able to reach Lampersveldt before Neda's Feast," Torry tells the man flatly.

"I'll never understand how you read those things," Postas remarks vaguely, but he's immediately cut off by the messenger.

"Not possible," the messenger yawps. "Truzi will need the posters in place well before the fall equinox. The delegates for the summit will have begun arriving for Saman. He'll need you in time for Neda's Feast at the latest."

"No can do," Torry says, smirking. "I'm traveling with a tenderfoot here." She inclines her head toward Postas who does his best not to look surprised while he feels as though pinwheels have just begun turbining in his eyes. "I'll have to indoctrinate him in the conventions of the amber road as we go. You can tell Truzi I'll be there by Saman's Feast." She jams the lotería disks back in the capsule and hands it back.

The messenger looks like he's about to say fifty things at once, but then literally throws up his hands and hastens away toward the library.

Torry and Postas exchange a glance.

"You're going to uproot me just like that?" Try as he may, Postas can't stop his eyebrows quivering with a fervor that belies any objection. "I have a function here, you know."

"Don't worry. Now that the carousel's part of the Shah's hoard, it'll never stop revolving."

Their first night out, after they'd traveled several hours along the amber road, Torry and Postas detoured along a certain branching path at Postas' suggestion. After several minutes, they came upon a palisade wall about ten meters high enclosing an area about as big as a gristmill. Postas had remembered the place as one he'd previously traveled to with some of his friends one evening in the middle of a peaceable season many years ago.

Torry and Postas found the single door to the place unsecured, so naturally they went inside. It was quite dark at this point, but Torry had brought a flaming torch from the ambulant portmanteau, and she played it about. What Postas had recalled about the place seemed still to be. There was an enormous iron cannon mounted upon a timber framework stretching up as high as a lookout tower. Shadows of collapsing pillars crashed down around them as Torry lofted her torch. The cannon itself was inclined directly toward where the moon shone, and the thing's bore could have accommodated a small hut.

"I'll bet this one requires a lot of fodder," Torry had remarked.

Next to the cannon framework, and allotted fully half the substantial area of the palisade enclosure, was a child's playground slide. It was about as tall as the hut that would have fit in the cannon. It had a short sturdy ladder up to the howdah, the small enclosure where one comports oneself for sliding, and atop that a little pennant with a camelopard on it. The slide itself was helical, and it made two full twists before it would have spilled a merrymaking joyrider to the dirt below.

The palisade and its contents dated from the initial expedition of the Shah's representatives to Terra Termina, the same expedition that had built the library, and these items clearly had never made it the rest of the way. Apparently, the trailblazers had had both invaders and progeny in mind. The invaders never arrived, and neither had the intended progeny until just a handful of seasons ago when the HomeHub had finally been established with its mater and pater.

While Torry was examining the cannon, Postas had wandered over to a sheltered area beneath the slide and had let out an excited whoop. What he'd found there were the remains of an item which had also been abandoned some time before. The object was tarnished, and the papery bits of it were warped and obscured, but when he brought it over to show Torry, she knew just what it was.

"Janbiya lamp," she'd said sullenly, and spat in the dirt. "Even though it's already ruined, you should get rid of it," and she went back to her inspection.

A janbiya lamp is a lot-casting device, normally constructed and used by secretive factions with sedition on their minds. It's meant to reveal the will of God, as that will pertains to assassination. It consists of a paper shade with fins cut into the top, balanced upon a small lantern. At the center of the assembly is an arm made of some springy fiber upon which a jujube thorn or a sharp piece of wood or metal is mounted. The tensile arm is held in place with a piece of twine. On the paper shade, spaced evenly around, are the inked or painted likenesses of four to six high-ranking officials of the Shahdom, possibly including the Shah himself. As the heat from the lantern radiates, it slowly rotates the shade. Eventually, the twine is worn down by the heat. It releases the arm, and the barb pierces the paper shade. The person whose likeness is so pierced, selected as they are by Providence, then becomes the object of the assassination conspiracy.

What Postas had decided not to tell Torry upon observing her reaction was that he and his friends had themselves constructed this janbiya lamp with materials they'd brought along from Terra Termina all those years ago. They certainly had neither the resources nor the wherewithal to implement a conspiracy to assassinate either the Shah or the personnel of any of his HomeHubs. Postas and his friends hadn't yet donned the vestments of adulthood at that time, and the errand of theirs to the palisade enclosure had itself been the stuff of youthful thrillseeking. If anything, their motivation for crafting the lamp was rooted only in some juvenile impulse to subversion.

Postas had reflected that Torry took this sort of thing quite a bit more seriously than he ever had. Truth be told, while the influence of the Shah is felt in Terra Termina, if nothing more than in the taxes it levies, the place is a post so remote that Postas rarely had cause to consider whether he was inclined to conform to the laws of the realm or not.

Still, all these weeks into their journey, Postas supposes not unreasonably that Torry holds his life in her hands, and it's subtly affected their dynamic. She's shown him the most practicable ways to obtain meals, the protocols for encountering and interacting with other travelers they happen to meet, and generally how to pass safely through this largely unregulated countryside. On more than one occasion, they'd encountered mounted aswaran units of the Shah. The aswaran had been captivated by the ambulant portmanteau, and several of them had dismounted and studied the conveyance from every angle. If none of them had recognized Torry personally, they at least understood her function, apart from which she had official equipment to show them if necessary. They knew to leave her alone. Postas couldn't imagine how he'd have handled the aswaran if he'd been by himself. Possibly they'd have simply ignored him, but possibly they wouldn't have either.

Postas had ventured to ask Torry at one point if she reckoned the janbiya lamp from the palisade enclosure had really been used by conspirators, or if it wasn't perhaps something someone had constructed as a sort of toy or a joke. She'd laughed and explained that it wouldn't have mattered. If the aswaran, for example, had found it among a traveler's luggage, they'd have extracted confessions and put the party to death then and there. She went on to explain that any protective structure, such as a partnership, a village, or the Shahdom itself, will have at least one sacrosanct totem, the transgressing of which will rightly spell doom for the transgressor. In her own case, she explained, it was the walkabouts her tribe required of anyone capable of climbing to the top of a spiny urchin tree and back down. Torry'd made the climb as a child as had several of her peers, she'd recounted, and if she hadn't proceeded with a walkabout at that point, she'd have been ritually put out of the village and probably wouldn't have lasted long after that. Instead, she'd become a leader of her tribe. Postas had walked alongside her for almost an hour in the near-dark after that, hoping she couldn't somehow sense the disquietude he imagined as exuding from his very pores.

Another several weeks along, and they'd reached a village from which Lampersveldt was a ten day's journey. They'd arrived on the eve of Neda's Feast, and so nearly everyone was engaged either in preparing manti in the shape of Neda's bell, or in garlanding houses and stables with lengths of ribbon which had been precisely hand-tattered, as was the robe Neda wore. Almost immediately, they'd been asked to stay and to eat by a man wearing a linen covering which draped his head and swept the ground on all sides. The covering was a deep red, a color you'd never have seen the like of in Terra Termina, and the only opening apart from the one you'd remove it by was a mesh-covered rectangle through which you could see the man's mouth.

They'd accepted and gone with the man, Navid, to his home. Once they'd all gotten inside, into a small vestibule, Navid had removed his covering and left it on a peg next to several identical ones. In a dining area just inside was a rough wooden table around which five men sat in plain cotton tunics, just like the one Navid wore. The room was ill-lit and unadorned, though a single sheaf of grain was nailed to one of the ceiling's crossbeams. Torry noticed it there, Postas observed, and she'd emitted a barely-audible expiration which he'd recognized by this point as a sign of disdain.

Once they'd gotten settled, introductions were given, and a pottage had been handed around, the customary exchange of tidings and fabrications was made. Though they hadn't mentioned their official business, Torry had explained that she and Postas were bound for Lampersveldt, and that they'd likely remain there for the duration of the forbidding season. The fall equinox, after all, was mere weeks away.

As the evening progressed, Navid had told them the latest news of Lampersveldt. It seemed that a highly positioned outlaw, Capo Deshban, had been recently apprehended nearby by an aswaran patrol, and that he was now being held at HomeHub Emzadi there.

Deshban had led them on a chase which had lasted the better part of a day. The patrol had missed a chance at taking him by complete surprise, and he'd made off toward a known shrine of refuge. If nothing else, he'd have been better able to defend himself there, but it wasn't to be. The patrol had reached him at the last moment. Quarry and pursuers had been within view of the shrine when the pursuit was ended.

"Travelers report having recently spotted a vine satyr of the sort Deshban and his confederates have been known to leave," Navid remarked, carefully pouring some dark condiment onto his plate. "It's about two days out toward Lampersveldt, so they say, not far from the amber road in a broad field beyond a marked tree. Perhaps you'll see it along your way."

"Maybe so," Torry said thoughtfully. "I wonder if it appeared after Deshban was arrested."

"I trust it had," Navid said, and sipped the stuff from his plate. "I'm confident we've had some Native Orphans, Deshban's set as they call themselves, pass through the village in both directions since, though I'm sure Speaker Truzi would have us believe it'll all be put to an end with Deshban."

"Well, Truzi's nothing if not systematic," Torry pronounced, and pushed her plate back a fingerlength.

"I hope never to meet the man," Navid said, and went back to his dinner.

It was an odd meal, which only became more subdued as it progressed. It seemed all the more cheerless against the backdrop of the feast day preparations going on about the village. The other men rarely said anything, and only spoke to each other in low tones without any sort of gesture. Torry and Postas were invited to stay the night in a small larder off the dining area. Torry woke early in the morning to Postas staring at her from a hairsbreadth away.

"Let's be off," she said.

They managed their exit without waking anyone. Once they'd gotten outside, Torry showed Postas what she had, clasped gently in her hand. It was the sheaf of grain from the dining area. Apparently she'd torn it from the crossbeam sometime in the night. She asked

Postas to give her a leg up, and she tacked the sheaf directly above the front door, leaving it nearly hidden under the eaves.

"If the aswaran go door-to-door here, as I suspect they may, they're going to want to know what sort of people live in this cottage."

She rebuffed Postas' questions, and the pair made their way to the edge of the village to where they'd hidden the ambulant portmanteau in some undergrowth.

An hour out of the village, and they were traveling along some low-lying marshland which would give them a chance to fuel up and ride for a bit. The pair waded cautiously into the marsh with a wooden cask apiece until they came upon a shallow trench of pooling water whose surface swirled with unctuous coppery colors. They knelt and steadily dredged the trench, carefully collecting a mass of moldering vegetation and the stagnant miry slurry it was pickled in.

Back at the portmanteau, Torry threw open the grate of the conveyance's cast iron firebox and gingerly emptied the contents of the casks inside, securing the door after. She took her time examining the steering linkage, following the weblike matrix of struts and bushings up to the helm. Satisfied, Torry struck a fire-steel in her tinderbox and set light to a wooden splint. This she inserted into a flanged opening in the firebox no bigger than a lot-casting stone. The flame took, she shuttered the opening, and peered through a small circular crystal pane. Inside, a spectral blue-green flame hovered and seemed to flit over the surface of the boggy pulp. Torry and Postas took to the coxswain's pew, the throttle was rejiggered, and they were off once again along the amber road, this time as passengers.

In the middle of their second day out from the village, at this very moment in fact, Postas spots the marked tree. The marking is disguised as a winding scar along the trunk, as when a tree sustains a lightning strike. Still, the blemish is too angular. Too artistic. Anyone who actually observes it can discern that the marking is rendered by a human hand guided by human conceptions about lightning.

"I guess we'd better take a look," Torry says doggedly.

They secure the portmanteau within a stand of trees. Torry slings her supply sack, and they push through the underwood. After several minutes, they come to a ravine which they clamber down, and then they stop to rest a moment at the bank of a creek which is more rocks than water.

"Some years ago," Postas muses, "A vintner who'd stopped in Terra Termina described a vine satyr he'd seen on his travels. He'd said the sight of it put him in touch with obscure convictions, whatever that meant. I've wanted to see one ever since."

"Sounds like he was ready to disappear into the woods with Deshban and his Orphans," Torry scoffs. "Anyway, strictly speaking, vine satyrs are illegal. They wouldn't be so bad in themselves. No one would be particularly bothered if I or anyone felled a few trees and floated them out to sea, for example, but vine satyrs have become an emblem of groups like the Native Orphans, and other movements they emerged from. On the one hand, constructing a vine satyr is something like an act of poaching or trespass, but on the other it's a direct subversion of the Shah himself. It's a code of conspiracy and revolution."

"I still want to see one," Postas says, and crosses to the other side of the creek.

The pair maneuver through another stand of thick woods on the other side of the ravine which then gives way abruptly to a vast tract of grass-covered open land. For a moment, Postas is struck dumb. Growing up in Terra Termina, the most grass he'd seen in one place was only that which filled an ornamental lawn in the library courtyard. There's a broad gently-sloping hill he tentatively makes his way down, and so he spots the thing before Torry does. The woods curve around to the north and there in the grass, about a banqueting hall's length from the trees, is the vine satyr.

The figure is enormous, both in height and in general magnitude. The armature on which it's built is comprised of entire treetrunks and large branches. These are swathed and fettered with prodigious lengths of vine, stalk, and green vegetation. The figure is adorned with a profusion of wildflowers in a variety of colors and shapes, and then there's the figure itself. It's in the form of a crosslegged man with one palm raised to the sky and the other resting on the ground. It has two large curving horns atop its head twisted precisely from clumps of desiccated brown vine, and its beard is a cluster of shaggy brush. Its hooves are roughly hewn from green wood.

The figure prevails there inscrutably in the dazzling sunlight with only the sounds of insects, birds, flowing water, and the wind all around. Postas can't quell the feeling of exultation welling in his stomach and spreading to his limbs. This should have been something he and his friends of youth had found on one of those magic-charged nights afoot. It would have changed who he was, Postas thinks. He laughs resoundingly. There's no one in sight, they'd met no one on the amber road for the better part of a day, and yet here is this artifact which must have taken many people quite a long time to construct. It achieves a confoundingly strange effect.

For the past several minutes, enmeshed in his admiration of this effigy, Postas has lost track of Torry, but he's heard her rummaging with something on the other side of the figure, and now he sees a thin wisp of smoke rising over the opposite side. Dashing around to her side of the figure, he sees Torry thrusting her torch yet again into a small hollow where the flame immediately catches on some dry vegetation.

Postas is dismayed to be sure, but he finds he is incapable of doing or saying anything even to *try* to stop her. He stands mute. Once Torry's finished with her ministrations, the effigy has begun to burn in earnest. Orange flames caress the satyr's legs. Its abdomen is already a crackling furnace.

Torry insists that they camp just inside the woods that night and take turns keeping watch to see if anyone approaches the figure, but by the time the sky begins to lighten in the east, no one has. The place seems as desolate as it had the previous day.

In the morning, the vine satyr is a tumbledown collection of charred timber, ash, and a substantial pile of smoldering cinders. Torry approaches carefully, and still sees no one apart from Postas in any direction. She gives a blackened length of timber which hadn't fully given way a push with her foot, and the remaining structure collapses on itself. All that's left is a scorched pit.

Surveying the scene a final time, the pair start up the low hill, back in the direction of the amber road. The wind stirs the grass, and the grass shimmers winkingly in the morning sun.

Light that's the color of sanctified statues makes the pathway look like it isn't all there. Here, at the top of a small declivity, one can see how the track skews among the sculpted features of the large public greenspace.

This is one of the realm's nocturnal gardens, decreed by the Shah. Here, the gates don't open until sundown, and the place is closed to the public during daylight hours. It's meant to be viewed after dark. Night-blooming plants have been specially selected throughout, and the sculptures and statuary are designed with moonlit surfaces in mind.

From place to place across the tableau, there are obscure twists of movement where various transactions, conflicts, and recitals are carried out by those who are abroad this night. Torry and Postas are among them.

"A branching footpath like this one is the best place for the sort of navigational augury you were asking about the other night," Torry opines, and crouches down to examine the pavement cracks, huffing a visible steam of breath. "Lime mortar. We had these types of paths back of the settlement where I grew up. Even now, seeing a lime mortar path like this instills a kind of transcendent glimmering in me. Too bad we're past all the vernal rites of the turning for now, and the peaceable season's some time off. It's a *vernal* glimmering, this one."

Torry stands, pulls her patchwork mantle closer over a tunic which says "SOVEREIGN PLAYBILL" across the front, and rummages in the bulky supply sack slung about her shoulders.

Torry and Postas had arrived in Lampersveldt some weeks ago now. Having approached along the amber road from the vast emptylands they entered the city, as most do, through Fathoms Gate. They were met there by an official detachment sent by Truzi from HomeHub Emzadi, but there were also a throng of wharf cocks, as often there are in Lampersveldt at any event which smacks anything of ritual, ceremony, or gravity. While others of their number contributed to the general spectacle, three wharf cocks swaddled in colored crêpe overspilled the entry gates and whirled some way beyond, memorializing the tallfires which used to haunt the emptylands outside Lampersveldt, careening across the landscape like tournedos on a saucy platter. The crêpe of the wharf cocks was speedwell-blue, gourd-green, and flint-black, signifying each of those spindly infernos of auld.

Uh-oh. Any time we mention Truzi's name in Lampersveldt, as we just had there, he can gaze through his Glass Slattern and put his "lord-word" in. He can broadcast over items of discarded refuse (leather scraps, broken pottery, fruit rinds, and so forth) in public areas anywhere within the city gates. Given the chance, he almost always does too. I'm not sure how he accomplishes anything else with the hours of the day. In any case, it's not that he can read our thoughts, spy on us other than being generally aware of the name-use, or have any context for what he's about to express, but that's never been a problem for him before (Glass Slatterns, by the bye, are blown glass chamber pots, tinctured a translucent greeny-blue color with the addition of copper filings to the molten sand during the rendering. They're globular, and in the rough shape of a stocky figure with heavy jowls, broad shoulders, and meaty forearms. They were promotional items gifted by Satrap Bank and Brokering Consortium to new depositors who opened an account with five sigloi in the peaceable season of '23).

Truzi's accomplished something wholly unique with his Glass Slattern, honestly, and now he has a relationship with it which cannot be readily undone. There happens to be a castoff mutton bone to the side of the footpath Torry and Postas are traveling along, through which they overhear the following broadcast.

Oh, hello. It's your Minister of Licit Affairs piping in and up. I've nine delegates here now, my skriddis. You've probably seen us abroad either along The Fives, or in one of our canton's more closeted chambers. Only one delegate to go for a quorum, and then I'll be a lot less nameless and faceless than I've been. These glass eyes and plaster cheeks will warm

over with creature presence, and so it'll go. That's good news for most of
you.

Traaa-la-la-la mimsy-rah,
Silver in the crown, or the rats won't drown.
Traaa-la-la-la hearken-lo,
Swing a pot of embers, and cast them down.
Anyhow, please gaze upon HomeHub Emzadi if you haven't recently.
In preparation for the summit, it's been anointed with consecrated paint.
The canniest preceptors have performed their obscure calligraphy upon it
in hook-ends, broad virgules, and typographic barbs; runes tall as mega-
liths, daubed in violent line. The runes are chemically treated to lumi-
nesce steadily from "lantern" at dusk to "pyre" at the last moment of the
night. The luminance is cancelled only when the final acousticule of the
midnight minaret bell has flitted away to its bangarang burrow, only to
renew from the beginning of the next dusktime. If nothing else, it'll keep
the succubi at bay at least until Saman's Feast.

Traaa-la-la-la mimsy-rah,
Silver in the crown, or the rats won't drown.
Traaa-la-la-la hearken-lo,
Swing a pot of embers, and cast them down.
That's all, then, my skriddis. Farewells and flatworms to you all.

Without skipping a beat, Torry completes her supply sack rum-
mage, and comes away with a small ampoule of honey which she
commences to pour carefully onto a cluster of lime mortar pavement
cracks. A runnel branches slowly one way and then the other each
time it comes to a split. Torry nods and replaces the ampoule in her
sack.

"In the settlement where I grew up," she muses, "Just past some
gaming fields and along a glacier-scoured cauldron, you'd come to
another branch of that lime mortar footpath, only about as wide as a
fighter kite. If you walked along the footpath to the west, you'd come
to a dwarven length of palings, a stand of trees, and a few outlying
goat-hair tents beyond which the wildlands really began.

Right at the end of that footpath though, the paved surface was
cracked to pieces. Cracked, but not crumbly. On certain days when

you walked down to the end of the path, the conditions were just right, and there'd be tiers of luminous yellow and purple clouds back in the eastern sky over your childhood homestead.

On those days, the cracks of the footpath would vouchsafe to you small details of life, and of your personal future. They'd be small details, yes, but they might also be significant. The yellow-purple sky would shine on the footpath cracks, you'd examine how a transverse crack knits across two others, and you'd understand that you would one day break bread with a one-eyed man in a ruined fortress a thousand leagues away in place and time.

You'd get only a little at once from this footpath-crack augury, and you'd usually get it by surprise. For every nineteen trips down the path, there'd be one when you'd peripherally glance at those terminal cracks and get a little flash of something. A jagged hashmark of a crack would give you a hint about the emotional impression given off by an individual goat in the corral.

If you got a flash of something, you'd count yourself sanctified for that afternoon. As a token of sacrifice, you'd take a roundabout way home even when you could've caught a final game of boundscotch with your playmates if you'd taken the more direct route.

Then you'd walk idly among the tents on the periphery of the settlement, and you'd still get a sense through the trees of the . . . *pith* of that footpath and the open land it passes through. The trees were a filter. In some places there'd be a single layer of trees buffering the footpath from the outlying tents, and in others there'd be two or three layers. The pith of the crisscrossing footpaths would get more or less concentrated as you walked along. The *species* of buffer-tree made a difference too. Plane trees brought out the wistfulness of the place, whereas cypress brought out the festiveness, and cedars brought out the enigmaticalness."

Postas levels a measured look at her. He'd nearly forgotten what an intense aspect Torry can conjure. The facepaint she wore while they traveled here from Terra Termina had been a holdover from her walkabout days. Now, washed clean of the paint, he's struck once again by the angle of her brows and the sway of her cheekbones.

"With something that smacks as much of open-air intuition as that does," Postas ventures, "I'm surprised you're not more in line with Deshban and those Native Orphan types."

"Careful," Torry murmurs, casting him an abrupt look, "Where and how you express things like that, even if it's just an unmoored thought of no particular intent. It's just basic statesmanship. Lampersveldt is not the amber road with no one around to hear for days at a time."

"Maybe I'm just restless in this place," Postas remarks morosely, "And no, honestly, I don't have much of a taste for statesmanship, or for this setup with . . . our host. I don't particularly care to name him again straightaway and have to listen to another broadcast."

"Yes, well, he is the pater of HomeHub Emzadi, and I'm a poster vendor in the Shah's employ. What else is there to be said?"

"He has a *family*."

"A HomeHub family is only definitional and titular. That's understood by all involved. Besides which, the child who lives with them is not his heir, and . . . our host knows that."

"Surely you're not obliged to share his bed." Postas can barely keep the quaver from his voice.

"I hope that's not what all this is really about."

"Of course not." Postas looks away.

"Anyway, if it makes you feel differently about it, Truzi's carnal tastes run to the classical end of the spectrum."

"Oh?"

"He is the scabbard, and I am the sword."

"Ah."

Uh oh. Here's Truzi again with his lord-word, this time from across a melon rind on a curbstone.

Tidings from the minaret are that the wooden homunculus is spindling faster than is the metal homunculus. Hark back to the last instance of that, and you'll come up with the forbidding season of '32. No, you didn't hear that wrongly, never mind the medium you're listening on. Yes, ice blazes. That's what the little elemental men in the box on the tower would warn us of, if you heed little men. In any case, I'll be staying indoors tonight. I've got three seasons of illuminated manuscripts to catch up on.

Laaa-da-da ty-ro say-fah,

Pour a pot of sugar down the barrow mound.

Laaa-da-da hie-here di-po,

Catch a fist of crickets for the piebald hound.

Please, if you happen to see him, kiss the legs of Drus Wym who's just arrived from HomeHub Hyssop. Now that Wym's here, we have the complement we require to proceed with Deshban's undoing. The ironworkers, carpenters, and rope-makers have surpassed themselves. It's going to be a real corroboree, come Saman's Feast.

Laaa-da-da ty-ro say-fah,

Pour a pot of sugar—

"Deceit! Misery! Ruin!" a wailing voice interrupts, all but drowning out the sound of the spheres themselves, and certainly obscuring whatever signoff was still coming across the melon rind.

Torry and Postas have just turned down the third branch of the footpath dictated by the honey runnel, and have happened abruptly upon this singular figure in the dark. A pair of latchkey urchins who'd been derisively throwing stones at the wailer loose a surprised yelp and hare away down a brambly side-path. The figure is standing atop a crumbling tiger statue, swaying precariously and trailing off into gibberish chatterings.

The figure has a womanly aspect, but is on the one hand so swaddled in sackcloth and on the other so transpierced with thorns, she is effectively androgynized.

"Hello!" Postas calls, "Is there anything we might help you with?"

The figure turns. Her face is a mosaic of thorn piercings. The thorns are long and thin, like those of the jujube bush, and each thorn is woven into the skin around her eyes and down her cheeks in a pattern of winding curlicues. There's brownish coloring around each pierce-point which is either dried blood or thorn sap. Her hands, the only other visible part of her anatomy, are similarly pierced. She turns and shuffles away through a narrow opening in a thicket.

"Alright, let's leave this place," Torry breathes. "That's put me off path-auguring anything for the Dispersed Treasurehouse in here. We should make our way over to The Fives. I may get another spoor of something there. As cold as it is, you'll probably want to catch the last beach fire of the season anyway."

"Penitent Abigail. That's her." Postas looks spooked.

"Hm?"

"Haven't you seen her before?" Postas asks, looking in the direction the figure disappeared. "She's always in that way, too. I don't know if that's really her name, but people say she was a confederate of Deshban's. The wharf cocks say it, yes, but . . . our host's company do too."

"Penitent Abigail Granary? As in the line of couscous and farina you see at the bazaar? Not likely. I don't think that woman can count her own fingers."

"Well not anymore she can't; no. She's the woman pictured on the label of those products, though. Those are thorns in the drawing on the package, not wrinkles on an old woman's face . . . Our host broke her mind in the pit Deshban now languishes in, and then named a line of household foodstuff after the incident so that she'd see it everywhere she went."

"Oh?"

"She's not regretful about her association with Deshban or the Orphans, though," Postas carries on. "Of that I'm sure. '*Penitent Abigail*' is just another element of the depraved backstory . . . our host fabricated. Just another aspersion on the poor woman. As if she isn't tortured enough."

"Our host may not be a particularly endearing or even honorable example of the genus," Torry ventures, "But this sounds exactly like the sort of thing a half-there wharf cock would come up with a few minutes before he nodded off from taking too much firedust."

By this time, the pair had reached The Fives. The Fives is an open-air maidan, a pedestrian mall, and it is the traditional domain of the wharf cocks. Approaching from the east, Torry and Postas survey the place. Dominating the maidan is the kidney-shaped lagoon of the wharf itself. There is neither sea nor slough within a skua's flight of Lampersveldt, and so many childhoods ago, the wharf cocks (or maybe their progenitors) gouged this faux-cove out of the parched and frangible dirt.

Here the cocks preen and swoop about their beach fires, casting firedust from the embossed leather purses slung about their shoulders. The sand of the beach is real enough, there's plenty of it to be had after all, and as usual three raging bonfires dominate the scene. The fires are colored with chemical dust, each one representing another of the tallfires. Even standing here at the periphery of The Fives tonight, the energy is palpable. Most wharf cocks cut off the arm-ends and leg-ends of their garments and wear the knotted-together ends like a tail. Many of this assemblage have done just that, and as they caper around the fires whipping their heads and whirling about, the errant knot-tails stir sparks and cinders from the flames.

To Torry's mulish chagrin, Postas is caught up in the excitement. Over his leather thong laceups, Postas is wearing a pair of cardboard "castoff shoes" which the wharf cocks themselves are permitted to make and sell. Now he joins the procession of tourist-types threading among the bonfires to the cacophony of rubber band tanburs and slide whistles, readying to commend his castoffs to the flames at the prescribed point. A particularly extravagant wharf cock with teased up hair and nacreous hazeglasses tosses a handful of iridescent crystals from a leather purse and commences in to crooning:

> The moon does gust as the birds do weep, and the cardboard shoes walk the Fives. Emzadi snickers from up the round hill, as the tallfires twine in the sky.

> Once was a time when you'd see the tallfires, spindling across the plain. One hissed flint-black, one speedwell-blue, and another crepitated gourd-green.

> In the Precedent Age of Combustive Knack, each tallfire patroned the wards. Now the chimneypot of 'Zadi bricky-ratchets 'cross the way, and flicks the castoff shoes to the sides.

> So, though you feel a heat-shimmer, see a snap of gray sparks, those old fires let pneuma alone. Let's sprinkle our dust, newly stock our trust in fire-colored fires in a threadbare gown.

Bulb-hair pearl-glasses then stands atop a wooden chest holding aloft a tattered loincloth that had been littering The Fives until only a moment before. The loincloth has a crude mouth and eyes drawn on it with a bit of charcoal.

"Attention, everyone! Let's hear what our Minister of Licit Affairs has to tell us all. If you will, please . . . SPEAKER TRUZI."

At mention of the name, the pater once again transmits his lord-word from wherever it is he's ensconced, verbalizing across the Glass Slattern. This time, as the broadcast progresses, the loincloth puppet manipulated by this spirited wharf cock mockingly mouths the words, all to the hoots and hurrahs of the other wharf cocks and to the uneasy amusement of everyone else.

As the display proceeds, Postas, who's rejoined an unimpressed Torry at the periphery gives her a cautious look.

"Why is it that anytime . . . our host speaks across the Slattern he uses those 'Traaa-la-la-la's and 'Laaa-da-da ty-ro's anyway? He doesn't punctuate himself that way in person."

"Yes, well, it's an artifact of using the Glass Slattern, as I understand. Something to do with a verbal approximation of the resonant frequency of the glass. I really can't understand why he's as taken with the medium as he seems to be."

"Especially when he leaves himself open to displays like this one," Postas says gesturing over to the farce still being enacted atop the wooden chest. "Anyway, have you managed to pick up the trail again? Get a hint of anything for the Treasurehouse thingy?"

"No, not using augury anyway. I chatted briefly with one of the wharf cocks though. Apparently there's a barrelhouse not far from here which isn't widely known. Evidently it attracts some unique clientele. I think we ought to go see it."

Torry and Postas follow a map the wharf cock carved for Torry on the spot as best they can. He'd hewn it with a pocketknife from a large unripe walnut in all planes in order to depict a passage along the stairways and angles of the town. They manage to find one landmark after another and make a couple productive backtracks until finally they find themselves outside a plain-looking door in an alcove with a small pictograph drawn on it as described. They knock, are briefly sized up from a sliding door-viewer, and are let in.

Inside, the light is wan and orange in the oily discharge from the lamps. The air has a texture and a pungency to it. There is a continual rumble of voices, noisy but indistinct, as if each speaker is conversing through a handkerchief. The wall is paneled timber all around, no windows, and the interior is about the size of a small churchyard. There are tables and benches running widthwise down either side of the room. Between every table is an enclosed compartment, each about the length and breadth of a table with its benches once again, and as tall as a wardrobe. There are eight of these enclosed compartments altogether, each with a different-colored "X" painted on the rough wooden door.

In the space of a minute or two as Torry and Postas watch, a somber-looking woman with an armful of scroll handles emerges from one compartment and crosses to another into which she disappears. The door of a third dimly-lit enclosure opens, emitting a man whose face is a spiderweb of blood runnels dripping viscidly onto his open shirtfront. The unsmiling man pauses to daub at his face and carefully closes the door behind him, but not before we glimpse another man lying prone on the floor and giggling, with several others situated on a bench alongside him.

Here and there, scattered throughout the room, there are amusements being deployed with daggers, and contracts being sealed with painful and inglorious oaths.

Torry's just secured a couple drinks and has taken a seat at one of the benches with Postas, when a lull falls over the room and a grotty impresario type steps onto a stage which is little more than a few empty casks with a board lain across the top.

"'Evening, all," the fellow rumbles, pausing to wheeze and to root in his ear. "Hope you've all saved enough equilibrium to enjoy a little music from a house favorite."

"Balls!" shouts a faceless someone from inside one of the enclosed compartments.

"They've braved the weather and our habitués in order to play here tonight. Do hail and hurrah . . . The Tinshop Quadrivium!"

The impresario makes way for a quartet of performers identically-dressed in striped tabards, white breeches, and flat straw hats of no practical use who, after playing a pitch on a reed whistle, commence to harmonize in euphonious modes which call to mind syrupy biscuits, angora blankets, and well-appointed hearths.

"Hey," Torry whispers. "Isn't that . . . our host?"

Indeed it is. Scrunched deep in an armchair off to the side of the room and not far from the stage, his lips even now pressed against the globular physique of his Glass Slattern, mouthing silent syllables, is the pater of HomeHub Emzadi and the man whose sovereign complex they'd been staying in for the past weeks.

"Guess he's decided to spend an evening abroad after all," Postas replies. "He's insinuating himself into yet another narrative, I see."

The pair watch the Tinshop Quadrivium persevere through their repertoire amidst a din of metal on wood and under a hail of indifference and general atmosphere. The themes of their songs are the celebration of life's earliest relationships, popular amusements of a time no one anymore recalls, and those things in which people used to find comfort and understanding, but haven't now for at least ten childhoods. No one in the barrelhouse really notices except for Torry, and Postas only notices her noticing.

"Lyrically, there's absolutely nothing objectionable about these songs," she whispers, "They're clearly meant to conjure a general feel of cheerfulness and nostalgia for something we've never experienced ourselves."

Postas gives an attesting shrug.

"Still, these songs are permeated with an underlying seediness. It's undeniable, as if they're trying to cover up some disgusting habit by throwing a cask of rose water over it . . . I think I'm going to curate this performance for the Treasurehouse. This place. Everything we're taking in right now."

"Can you do that?" Postas asks doubtfully.

Torry's gotten as far as removing the valise from her supply sack, fitting the stabilizing rod into the bottom of her black wooden box, and loading it with a stack of the tin effigy-sheets when the front door of the place blows open with a crash, and all the lights are extinguished in the gust. Oddly, everyone including the singers go almost completely quiet. There are still stirrings all around, and from across the room someone breathes "Ice blazes!"

Postas looks back through the door to the outside and sees there not ten paces away a hitching post which has been engulfed in a sarcophagus of translucent ice. A short distance down the road from there, he can make out a streetlamp which has been muffled in a glassy pillar.

"We'd better take the indoor route back to Emzadi," a nearby voice buzzes. "Don't care to seed one of those rimy shapes myself." In person, the voice is every bit as unctuous as it is in broadcast, but the acoustics of its closeness only make it all the more claggy. The pater himself, Glass Slattern cradled carefully in the crook of an elbow, leads Torry by the arm, and Postas trails in their wake.

Truzi conducts them through a dressing room and out the back of that, on through a short hallway and down a fungus-mottled stone stairway. Even now, Truzi tics as his name is used, but right now his hands are too full for levying his lord-word. From the stairway, they make their way in almost complete darkness through a system of root cellars, service tunnels, and sanitary sewers. After the time it takes to boil a pot of water, they emerge from a wooden hatch into a vast stone corridor which curves off circularly in both directions.

"Recognize it?" Truzi grins. "We're home. It's the sub-basement of HomeHub Emzadi. In fact, the eminent outlaw Capo Deshban is penned up just the other side of this wall."

"Yes, I don't imagine he's shifted quarters," Postas remarks dryly.

"Oh, but he will," Truzi counters. "Now that Vintner Wym is present, we'll be able to carry out Deshban's sentence. We'll do so on Saman's Feast."

"As soon as that?"

"According to proverb, 'The quicker a sinner is put to trial, the more benevolent is God's smile' . . . Anyhow," He says mischievously, "Let's go up to the gallery and have a bit of fun with him while we still can."

HomeHub Emzadi is built around a central atrium whose interior is lined in red-black tapestry from ceiling to foundation. Rooms and galleries for the HomeHub family and other officials branch from the atrium in the top floors of the building, and a similar structure branches for the helpstaff down below. When HomeHub Emzadi won the bid to execute the sentence of capital punishment on Capo Deshban, a sentence levied by the Shah himself, Truzi decreed the bare stone foundation of Emzadi for Deshban's prison. Deshban's been strung up there ever since by a single stout chain which runs the entire length of the atrium and which is anchored to the ceiling twenty meters up. Truzi has led an example of throwing refuse into the atrium and striking the chain at various places along its length with andirons, roasting skewers, and pruning shears, and several have followed suit. Truzi has seen to it that Deshban has been thoroughly harried during his doleful accommodation at Emzadi.

Postas never developed a stomach for this sort of thing and so even now, as Truzi and Torry begin an assault on the prisoner, hailing Deshban from high above with casks of washwater and tureens of week old stew, he nips down the back stairs and peers out into a partially sheltered courtyard garden he's been wont to while in. Even with the ice blazes visited upon the land, the courtyard has its denizens. Truzi is ever obsessed with the staving off of succubi, spectral women who are said to visit a pater's bed in the night in order to skim off some life, and so bags of human hair clippings are hung throughout the garden, tin pie pans whipped to wooden dowels clang together in the wind, and as Postas watches from across the courtyard, a member of the helpstaff carefully pours a stream of milk from a large pan, walking a path around the base of the tower which houses Truzi's sleeping quarters. Succubi are meant to be put off by the smell of the hair, the reflection from the pie tins, and the concept of the milk.

From the other end of the courtyard, a couple of the helpstaff pull a dilapidated chariot steadily along a covered arcade. The chariot is painted in peeling red and gold, and in its cab is a figure swaddled head to toe in muslin wrappings swaying gently to and fro.

Just as Postas is about to retire inside, he sees a flash from a thick cluster of ironwood about twenty paces away. He looks directly that way, and the flash comes again. A signal. As he minces over, he makes out a figure hidden within the branches. With a catch of breath he recognizes Penitent Abigail, or whoever she really is, the thorn-pierced woman, gazing at him from beneath the underbrush.

Once he's close enough, the woman extends her hand to him. She's holding a folded swatch of some ink-marked material that looks like vellum. Postas takes the proffered item and unfolds it. It's a loop of papery hide with four human figures painted on it. Postas thinks he recognizes the likeness of one of them, all HomeHub pater types, as one of their host's guests who have been arriving over the past several days. As Postas unfolds the object once more, a quiver of raw emotion flutters through him. There, in his hands, is the unmistakable likeness of the man he's come to hate, the pater of HomeHub Emzadi, with a ragged hole piercing the material over his likeness's chest.

"It's the shade from a janbiya lamp," he whispers tremblingly.

"And so you know what we must do. Very soon."

"We?"

"Meet me tomorrow at the time and place you first encountered me tonight. There will be others there who are prepared to see things through. Native Orphans."

Postas moves to hand the material back to her.

"Keep the shade," she says. "Keep it as a token of our mutual trust, and show it to no one else."

"I will come," Postas says without hesitation. "What is your name? Your real name?"

The woman, however, has already withdrawn into the undergrowth, has gone from there to wherever it is she hides herself.

His mind awhirl with the sphere of secret intent which has opened before him, Postas wants nothing more than to retire to his quarters for the evening, but Torry hears him passing by and calls to him from the greathall, bidding him come join them there.

Torry and Truzi are present, and so is a third man whom Postas doesn't recognize. Presumably it's Wym, the new arrival, and then Torry confirms this as she introduces them.

"Postas!" Truzi purrs. "Torry was just telling Wym and me about how the two of you'd come across a vine satyr on your travels." He glances at Wym with a smirk and places his Glass Slattern carefully on a low velvet-draped pedestal. "She told us what she saw you doing there early the next morning, though you thought she was asleep."

Postas looks over to Torry who appears to be about to say something, but then twists her mouth instead and leans cumbrously against a tabletop.

"She said you were supplicating it," Wym pronounces. "Even though the thing was brought to ash by that time, you were groveling there in front of it; pledging yourself to it."

"Torry told you this?" Postas is transfixed there by several conflicting impulses.

"Sounds a bit rustic, Postas," Truzi adds. "Especially having done the business bare-bottomed in a pointed cap!"

As Truzi starts cackling, Postas lunges toward him, upsetting the pedestal in the process. At one level, Postas hears Torry hastening to explain that's it's all just a foolish joke that Truzi had hatched a moment before he'd come into the room, and at another level he watches the Glass Slattern fall to the stone floor and shatter into a spray of jagged-edged rubble.

In that instant, Truzi stares immobilized at the sight of his broken prize, and it seems as though he's actually lost his faculty of speech altogether. Truzi's hands hover at his throat and his mouth gapes wide.

A moment later and Truzi's mouth is discharging a thin trickle of blood, some of which drips onto the haft of a metal rod, one from which a livery pennant has recently been stripped, protruding from Truzi's stomach. The other end of the rod is held by Drus Wym who lets the murdered pater crumple haphazardly in place. Wym looses his grip on the haft and takes firm hold of Postas.

"Murder!" He cries. "The Pater's been murdered!" From somewhere not far away, the shuffle of boots approaches from the turret stairway. "It's Postas Dendo of Terra Termina!" Wym shouts. "Summon witnesses! He's got the shade of a janbiya lamp hidden on himself!"

Hardly considering what she's doing, Torry crosses to them and sinks a heretofore concealed dagger deep into Wym's side. Wym lets fly a scream and spins away, collapsing next to the defunct pater.

"Down the far stairs," she commands, propelling Postas in that direction. "Now."

{COMMITMENT:}

Considering the alarum Drus Wym has raised, our pair have won a decent head start. Without expressly discussing it, both of them have decided that their one hope will be to make it to a known shrine of refuge some few hours' journey across the emptylands from Lampersveldt at the very edge of the woodlands which pick up from there. Their flight from the HomeHub itself comprises a splodge of ashen stone, dank passageway, and bland tapestry. On their way out through the stables, they encounter Maggom Faytho of Truzi's company, but he only tenders a distracted greeting to them on his way between errands. Apparently the hue and cry hasn't yet propagated to this far end of the complex.

Though the ambulant portmanteau is hitched in the partial shelter of one of the outbuildings, the ice blazes have had their way with it and the doughty conveyance is encased in one of the event's meteorological artifacts. Now the portmanteau's a guppy in a gristmill-sized fishbowl of frozen glaze, and there'll be no piloting it. Torry emits a resigned expiration and slings a diminished supply sack higher on her shoulders.

Even if there had been a marsh anywhere nearby, she reflects, it would have been frozen over. There's no motive slurry to be had for leagues.

The last of the outbuildings usher Torry and Postas through a half-used service hatch in the rampart wall, and they thread their way through a prodigious midden heap just outside the city. At last, they're in full view of the emptylands stretching away into the wilderness. At this end of Lampersveldt, the emptylands aren't strictly vacant. A plane of thick bracken and gorse blankets the land in a forbidding mantle, head-high in every direction, spreading away into the obscure. Patinaed as their branches are with the sleety gray muck of the ice blazes, the florae resemble nothing so much as the snapped and fractured implements of a defeated army fallen in place.

As they survey the prospect ahead, Postas ventures a query.

"So, had you changed your mind about Truzi and Capo Deshban at the last moment there?"

"No," Torry replies without wavering. "Wym's editing of the pater changed my mind for me. It changed my fate too, most probably."

"You had no other option?"

"None that I could reckon. What I'm perpetrating here is a crime of depleted prospect."

It's the depleted prospect, then, which unfurls before them. The pair are faced with two paths, the paths themselves a relic of the ice blazes of '32. These are the dual trailheads of a *phrastic ladder*, formed when the squall and flurry of those foregoing ice blazes scourged this swath of land all those years ago. A phrastic ladder forms when the binary tailwinds of an ice blazes butt up against a large obstacle such as the Lampersveldt battlements. The squalls slither through the thick vegetation, beating parallel paths about the length of a banqueting hall apart from each other, joining them at irregular intervals by three to five "rungs" which form corridors between the two main paths. The effect left in the storm's wake is that of a rickety ladder lain horizontally across the land, some formations of which can reach up to five kilometers long. The main wind current can cross back and forth across rungs of the phrastic ladder, crossflow's how the rungs are formed in the first place, and so any one segment of the path between rungs is usually more rugged and ill-formed than its parallel segment, making it considerably rougher-going than the other. For this reason, it's important for a beleaguered and time-pressed traveler only to cross those rungs which lead to a less-arduous trail segment than the one parallel.

This pair of paths have been named on a carven milestone set between them, Adam's Rib Aisle to the left, Ambleburg Attic Way to the right. In the lee of the milestone is something like a glass retort whose neck has been pushed into the soil. The accompanying lantern has long since gone out, but in the globe of glass one can just make out a collection of waxen lotería discs. Torry kneels down and squints at them.

"I'm glad of these, at least," she says. "A preceptor will have gone along at the cusp of the forbidding season and cast some conjectures about which path a traveler ought to take. The lotería here comprises snake, manti oven, and requital." She squints a moment more. "We'll go by Ambleburg Attic to begin with, then." The decision's made not a moment too soon either, for now a horn sounds from the ramparts and a host of Truzi's guard are seen ranked along the fortified wall. A series of shouted commands are barely audible over the gusty tumult, but there is no doubt that a sizable detachment of the guard are mobilizing in Torry and Postas' direction.

"One final thing," she remarks briskly, and withdraws a small cloth-wrapped bundle from her tunic. "I was saving this for Saman's Feast, but it may make all the difference now." Laying bare the wrapping, she reveals a heel of dark brown bread upon which overlays a thin even film of purplish fuzz. She breaks a corner off, places it carefully on her tongue and begins deliberately chewing it. "We won't want to eat much of this, but it will cue our senses. It'll help us draw on instinct we may not consciously know that we've cultivated."

Postas dubiously takes a proffered chunk of the bread and does the same as Torry.

In the intervening hour or two, the pair manage to stay out of eyeshot of their pursuers. There have been other retorts containing lotería roundels at each junction. Torry's spent less time parsing each one, presumably as the uncommon bread takes its effect and the parsing becomes more visceral. They've already crossed one corridor and kept on at another. To be sure, they've heard shouts on the wind, seen brief flashes of light possibly from somewhere behind them or along the parallel path, and have apprehended some indefinite sensation of a progressing chase. As they approach the fourth rung of the phrastic ladder, however, they hear a rhythmic clangor as if each member of an entire troop is beating the bottom of their own kettle in time. As they draw level with the corridor, they exchange the gaze of a company of some twenty men in the pater's employ about twenty paces away, lofting firebrands and gritting their teeth against the cold.

In that moment, Postas convulses as if hit with a cramp and sits down hard on the frozen ground. His gaze, directed upward now, is soon followed by the company of men who have momentarily halted in their advance.

Overspreading the gorse in their direction of travel, in fact shadowing about half the night sky somewhere between here and the edge of the forest, is the unmistakable likeness of a colossal vine satyr. Its horn-topped head rears on a fortress-sized trunk. The skyward-raised palm is all but completely obscured in the inky sleet-strewn ether.

Truly, the thing is too big for what it's made from. It should certainly have collapsed under its own weight. Apart from that, the forbidding season is the wrong time for a vegetal object such as this one not to be entirely withered and derelict.

Has the vine satyr just inclined its head? Have its limbs begun to stir? Postas' neck is seizing now as he pulls his attention back to Torry. She's standing there lantern-lit with no visible lantern casting its gleam. A sly smile blooms upon her face, and a red fox slinks unnaturally from the gorse and sidles up to her. Some short distance away, the company of men begin to disintegrate in the freezing rain, the icy beads pocking them away to nothing.

No surprise, really. This is a period piece, after all.

All that's left to note down now is the . . .

Full stop.

Made in the USA
Las Vegas, NV
04 June 2021